SO-BNX-750

MOJO
and the
RUSSIANS

ALSO BY WALTER DEAN MYERS

Fast Sam, Cool Clyde, and Stuff

MOJO and the RUSSIANS

Walter Dean Myers

The Viking Press   New York

First Edition
Copyright © Walter Myers, 1977
All rights reserved
First published in 1977 by The Viking Press
625 Madison Avenue, New York, N.Y. 10022
Published simultaneously in Canada by
Penguin Books Canada Limited
Printed in U.S.A.
1   2   3   4   5   81   80   79   78   77

Library of Congress Cataloging in Publication Data
Myers, Walter Dean, 1937–   Mojo and the Russians.
    Summary: A little bit of Mojo goes a long way for a
group of youngsters trying to protect their friend from
some suspicious characters.
[1. Voodooism—Fiction]   I. Title.
PZ7. M992Mo   [Fic]   77-23454
ISBN 0-670-48437-7

To Geraldine, Viola, Gertrude, Ethel, George and Imogene—the Martinsburg Gang

MOJO
and the
RUSSIANS

One

I was about ten feet in front of Kitty as we got near the corner. Thing about Kitty is that you have to beat her to the corners if you're going to win a bicycle race that she's in. See, she always slowed down more than most people when she got to the corners, but she made up for it when she got on the straight runs. The only people on the block that she couldn't beat were Kwami and me, but she was getting pretty close to me, too. Anyway, I was just about ten feet in front of her when we hit the corner. I reached down and switched into fifth gear and leaned into that corner perfectly and was just about ready to straighten out and really do it to the finish line when I saw this lady named Drusilla.

Well, I saw her and then again I didn't see her. That is, I didn't see her in time. All of a sudden she pops up from between these two parked cars and I jerked my handlebars so I wouldn't hit her. I think I shouted "watch out" or something like that, too. When I jerked the handlebars the bike started skidding and went right at her. I went over the handlebars and smack into the middle of the street. I hit so hard I thought I was going to pass out. I actually bounced!

All I could hear was this screeching and carrying on and I didn't want to turn around. An orange rolled past me and I figured I'd better take a look. I looked. Bad news.

Drusilla was lying between the parked cars with the sleeve of her blouse caught on the back fender of the car in front. The whole street was filled with oranges and broken eggs, and a broken bottle of Coca-Cola was still rolling toward the sidewalk. By this time the rest of the guys had come up from the corner and some of them, at least the ones who weren't standing around oohing and ahhing, were trying to clean things up.

I started to get up and felt this sharp pain. I looked down and saw that my pants were torn and I had skinned my right knee. Kwami and Anthony were helping Kitty up and she seemed to be okay. Her bicycle was turned over, too, and the front light was broken. No big deal. She never rides it at night anyway.

"IiiiiEEEEEEE!" When this scream came out everybody stopped what they were doing. It was this lady, Drusilla. "IiiiiiEEEEE!"

She was still between the two cars, only now she was halfway sitting up and staring at her hand. I went over to her and some adults came over, too.

"Call the hospital!" This tall guy was leaning over Drusilla like he was afraid that she had something catchy.

"I bleedin'!" Drusilla kept staring at her hand. I took a look. It was a small cut. My knee looked worse than her hand. I figured maybe she had bled about two or three drops at the most, and that had already dried.

Okay, now this police car pulls up and blocks off the street. This fat policeman gets out of the car and comes over to where we're all standing and comes up with this Adam-12 voice.

"Okay, give her some air! Give her some air!"

His partner comes over and starts looking at Drusilla to see if she's hurt, while the fat policeman pushes people away from where she's sitting.

"Okay, what happened?" The policeman that was looking at Drusilla's hand straightened up and took out his notebook.

"I come walkin' with me groceries when some fool come like a flyin' bat and knock me senses out and break me hand. That's what happened, and that's what God loves, the truth."

"You have any broken bones or anything?"

"Broken bones? What I look like, a doctor?"

"Well, how do you feel?"

"Like me hand is bleedin'." Drusilla looked at her hand again and let out a long piercing scream that even scared the policeman. "IiiiiiiEEEEEEE!"

"You know who hit you, lady?" The policeman was backing away as he asked her.

"I don't know the culprit. But if I find him out, I gonna make his tongue split like a lizard's and his eyes to cross." Drusilla stood up and looked around. "I'm gonna fix him good. Make his monkey ears fall off!"

"Any of you know who hit this lady?" The policeman never took his eyes off Drusilla.

At first I didn't say anything, but then I noticed everybody was looking at me.

"I hit her," I said.

"Well, if the lady doesn't want to prefer charges I think you should at least apologize."

"I'm sorry," I said to Drusilla.

"You not sorry now, you little hellion!" Drusilla lifted her finger and stuck it in my face. "But you're gonna be sorry 'cause you got evil in you! Look me in the eye so I got me a picture of you in my mind."

Now you got to see Drusilla to know that looking her in the eye is not a cool thing to be doing. She wasn't ugly or anything, just spooky looking. She was about the color of light coffee and her hair was half black and half grey and it kind of stuck out all over her head. When she brought her face close to mine I could smell her breath. It smelled like a deserted building. Then she got these little hairs growing out of her chin, see. She's not really ugly, but these little hairs don't do a lot for her. Two of them are white and straight and one of them is black and wiggly.

"I'm gonna fix you good," she says. She was almost cackling as she spoke. Then she turned around and picked up some of the stuff that had fallen out of the bag she had been carrying when I hit her and went off.

"There goes a strange one," the policeman said to me. "But you're lucky—she could have been hurt badly. If she had, you'd be in trouble now. Better be more careful how you ride that bike. You don't want to hit anyone else."

"The only way my man is going to hit anybody else with that bicycle is to pick it up and throw it at them." That was Kwami. "He can be trusted 'cause his machine is busted."

I looked over to where my bicycle, or what was left of it, was laying. Spokes here, spokes there, the fender twisted around the gears. What a mess. Kwami lifted it by one handlebar and the chain fell off.

"You'd better check yourself out, and check yourself steady"—Kwami slapped his palms together like he was giving himself five—"because that old witch done got you already."

The cops made us pick up all the stuff on the street—
the oranges, eggs, and the broken glass—and put it in a
trash can, and then they left. I got my bike over to the
stoop and took a good look at it.

"Can it be fixed?" Wayne came over. He was already
peeling one of Drusilla's oranges.

I just kind of shrugged because I didn't want to say
that it couldn't be fixed, but I sure didn't see how it
could be.

Kitty brought her bike over, and everybody came
around the stoop.

"You were lucky, though," Wayne said. "If she had
been hurt bad you could have been arrested. They might
have even put you in jail, or something."

"Don't be stupid, Wayne," Kitty said. "They don't
put kids in jail. All you would get is a fine."

"How you figure he's lucky, man?" Kwami took off
his left sneaker to shake out the pebbles. "She told you
what she's gonna do to you. She gonna make you tongue
split like a lizard's. Your ears are gonna fall off, your
nose is gonna turn to jelly, your eyes are gonna cross,
your head gonna spin around backward, and then some
bad stuff gonna happen to you."

"She can't do nothing," I said.

"What!?" Kwami jumped up. "What?! She can't do
nothing? Don't you knew she's Long Willie's girl friend?
And don't you know she came from Louisiana? And
don't you know she's a Mojo lady?"

"I heard all that."

"You heard it and don't believe it?" Kwami was still holding his sneaker in his hand.

"I seen this picture once where a Mojo man turned three people into zombies and then this . . . "

"Why don't you shut up, Wayne?" I gave Wayne a dirty look.

"Don't be mad at Wayne," Kwami said, sitting back down. "He didn't put no fix on you."

"Hey, man, what happened to your bicycle?" It was Judy Van Pelt.

"Hey, Judy, I don't mind you coming all the way down here to see Kitty—that's all right." Kwami leaned back against the stoop. "But I keep telling you that ain't no white girl supposed to be goin' around saying 'hey, man' all the time."

"What happened to your bicycle?" Judy asked, sitting down and ignoring Kwami.

"I had a slight accident," I said.

"Now you got a slight bicycle," Wayne said.

"Shut up, Wayne."

"What happened, Kitty?" Judy asked again.

"Dean and me were racing around the block and he hit this Mojo lady. You ever see this tall, light-skin lady that looks like . . . "

"Like a bad dream," Kwami inserted.

"Like she's undernourished or something?"

"Uh-uh."

"Well, anyway, she's supposed to be a Mojo lady and she said she was gonna fix Dean."

"I don't believe in people fixin' other people and things. That's just for television."

"You don't believe it because you're white," Kwami said. Kwami and Judy didn't get along very well. Judy was this white girl who used to hang out with Kitty all the time. She was really okay, but Kwami always seemed to have it in for her.

"I knew a lady said she was going to fix this guy who owned her building, this is when I lived in Virginia," Judy said, still ignoring Kwami, "and said she was going to fix him so he'd break his leg. She went through all these spells and humming and what not, and he never did break his leg."

"That's 'cause that stuff isn't real," I said.

"Of course he did die the next week, but his leg was fine."

"I don't believe that," I said.

"He didn't believe it either until everybody left his funeral and he was still there." Kwami put his sneaker back on. "Old Drusilla's probably home right now cooking up some roots. That's how they fix you. They cook up some roots and put some hair in it and say some Mojo words over it and then boil it on the stove. The more they heat, the more you beat."

"Heck, he didn't mean to hit her. She wasn't looking where she was going, that's all," Kitty said. "And all she got was a little jive cut."

"Hey, Dean, you know that catcher's mask you got

last year?" Wayne asked, looking like he just got a bright idea.

"Yeah?"

"Well, if anything does happen to you, will you tell your mother to give it to me?"

"Hey, Wayne." I stood up right in front of Wayne so he could see I wasn't fooling around. "Look, why don't you just shut up before I have to knock you out?"

"Don't knock *him* out," Kwami said. "Drusilla's the one that's going to put the Mojo on you."

"Kwami, look, I am not afraid of any Mojo or anything else like that. Okay?" I said. "Now will one of you people help me get my bike upstairs before my father gets home?"

"Hey, Dean, I got an idea," Kitty said. "Why don't you tell Willie what happened, and how it was an accident, and get him to talk to Drusilla for you?"

"Yeah, maybe I will."

"The only other thing I ever heard or saw about putting spells on people was this lady that told the mailman down home how to get a spell off of himself," Judy said to Kitty. "This lady had put a spell on him for kicking her dog, and this other lady told him to go out at midnight and swallow two live tadpoles under a full moon."

"Two live tadpoles under a full moon?" Kitty looked at Judy. "Then what happened?"

"Nothing happened to him for a whole week."

"What happened after a week?"

"He died."

"From the frogs?"

"It was the third full moon of the year, on a foggy night. He was driving along the highway and he heard this awful sound screeching and screeching at the back of his car. He stopped the car and got out to look around . . . "

"Then what happened?"

"Then he got hit by a truck."

"Let's go over to see Willie."

That's how the whole thing got started. I hit Drusilla and she's talking about putting some kind of spell on me. I didn't do anything that bad to her, but as Kitty said later, you can't tell how Mojo people think. When people start going around and talking about putting spells on people, it's serious.

Kwami had seen Long Willie in Joe Ferguson's Billiard Parlor and Barbecue Joint, but I thought it would be better to wait for him on his stoop.

"Yeah, you're right," Kwami said. "I can just see Long Willie all set to bite down on a juicy barbecued rib . . . "

"With Red Devil hot sauce . . . " added Kitty.

"Right," Kwami went on, "and you come busting in saying how you almost killed his woman in a hit-and-run accident."

"I didn't almost kill anybody," I said, trying not to get mad. Kwami had a way about him that could really get next to you sometimes.

"That's what you say," he went on. "I remember a guy got hit by a car one day on the Fourth of July, and he died three years later."

"Kwami, if you ran as fast with your legs as you do with your mouth you'd be one fast dude." Kwami was always putting people down, giving their ego a little nasty nudge. And he didn't have to, either. He wasn't any uglier than anyone else, or dumber, or even fatter. If he were you could say, okay, so he's got to be putting people down before they put him down, or something. But Kwami was cool. He was a real good basketball player. He ran track on the varsity and he was good with the books. But if anything went down to make you think that you were tight with Kwami—right away he'd start putting you down. That was his way. He wouldn't even say "Good morning" and stuff like that. He'd say something stupid like "How come you bothered to get out of bed this morning?" Things like that.

Anyway, he sat there for a while and then he looked as if he saw something down the street. He looked, and then he turned away and looked again real quick, like they do in the movies.

"Who that?" Kwami jumped off the stoop and looked down the street again. His eyes opened wide and his hand went to his mouth. "Here come Drusilla with a Mojo doll that looks just like Dean!"

We all jumped up and turned toward where Kwami was looking and started backing away.

"I don't see Drusilla," Judy said.

"No, but she might be around the corner," Kwami said, falling to his knees and laughing. Kwami fell to the ground and started rolling around the sidewalk. Judy started giggling and so did Kitty and Leslie. Everybody thought it was really funny. Everybody except me, that is.

"What's so funny about that?" I asked.

"You said you weren't scared." Kwami sat up. "Didn't you say you weren't scared?"

"I'm not scared."

"Then how come when I said I saw Drusilla you jumped up so fast you almost left your eyeballs on the stoop?"

"Oh, sweat." Judy grinned one of her wide grins. "He said you almost left your eyeballs on the stoop."

"I heard what he said," I said. "I just wanted to get up and see what he was looking at, that's all."

"My man jumped up so fast his shadow had to do a double take to see which way he went." Kwami gave himself five. "His heart was beating so hard I thought his chest had hiccoughs."

"Man, get out of here." I tried to look nonchalant. "I told you I'm not afraid of no Mojo."

"You don't believe in Mojo?" Kwami got right next to me and opened his eyes wide as if he were afraid.

"Haven't you ever heard of noise pollution, Kwami?"

"You don't believe in Mojo, right?"

"I didn't say that."

"Then you do believe in Mojo?"

"Maybe."

"Ain't no maybe, baby. Be strong or wrong 'cause you done heard the gong. Do you or do you not believe in the magical powers of the mystical Mojo which can tear you up in more terrible ways than you can possibly imagine and make you want to find a deep hole to crawl in and never be seen again? Do YOU believe, Michael Dean, also known as Mean Dean who made the Scene? Do you *believe?*" Kwami cupped his hand around his ear as if he were going to have trouble hearing me.

"I guess I believe."

"You GUESS! Is that your best? A guess? You got to be jiving."

"Okay, so I believe, now shut up."

"Dean, you in big trouble." Kwami sat back down and lowered his head. "I feel sorry for you, son."

"I think if you talk to Willie you won't have any problems," Leslie said. "Willie's okay.

"Here comes Willie now." Leslie nodded toward the corner. It was Willie all right, just walking easy the way he always did.

"Hey, Willie, what's happenin'?" I stood up and tried to smile a little. I have trouble smiling sometimes. I read in a book that the best smiles are when your teeth show a little, but everytime my teeth show it looks to me like I'm hurting someplace.

"Hey, fellows, how's it going? I'm so tired I could only wrap one lip around one of Joe Ferguson's choicest barbecued ribs."

"How's your new job?" I asked.

"Move over, boy," Willie gestured with his long hands, and me and Kwami slid down the stoop a little. "It's hard. Working ain't never easy unless you play in a band or play some sports. Anything like that is easy. But the kind of work I do is real hard and I ain't even supposed to talk about it."

"You still working up at the college?" Kwami asked.

"Yeah, but I can't give you kids no details."

"How come when you clean up you have to put the garbage in a—what did you call that thing again?"

"A shredder."

"Yeah, a shredder?"

" 'Cause everything I work with is top-secret government work." Willie picked his teeth with his fingernail. "They had to investigate my whole background before they even interviewed me. Nothing but top-secret stuff."

"What they do with the stuff after it's shredded?"

"They got to burn it, then."

"What do they do there that's so top secret, anyway?" Kitty asked.

"I'd love to tell you, honey, but I can't." Willie looked up and down the street and lowered his voice to a whisper. "It got something to do with a new secret weapon they trying to develop. If they get this one down right there won't be no more wars and stuff, you know."

"How come?"

" 'Cause all they have to do is take this thing out to the desert and shoot it at a rock, see, and the rock is gone. No trace, nothing. It don't make no noise and you can't see it coming. Zap. Bye-bye. It's all over. When the enemy see that, they *got* to give it up and start negotiating."

"It sound a little like Mojo to me," Kwami said, nudging me.

"Oh, yeah." I swallowed hard. "Say, Willie, I need a little favor."

"How much?"

"Look, I had an accident today, see, and I hit this woman."

"You got to be a man and face your medicine," Willie said. "That's how you become a man, by facing your medicine."

"You better learn that, Dean, in case somebody turns you into a frog or something." Kwami looked up in the air.

"Come on, Willie." I put my arm around Willie's shoulder. "You know, if I thought you needed a favor—"

"I got to go on downstairs right now. But you come around in an hour and tell me what's your problem, and I'll see what I can do about it."

"In an hour?"

"Yeah, what time is it now? Six o'clock. Come around about seven."

Willie stood up and stretched and went down into the basement where he had an apartment. Kwami looked at me and I just shrugged.

"Hey, man." Judy Van Pelt nudged me with the toe

of her sneaker. "You better hang around."

"Yeah, I guess so."

"I think you better bust on down to his pad now before Drusilla gets her stuff going. You might knock on his door and go to say something and your tongue fall out or something," Kwami said.

"Tell you the truth," Judy said. "I do remember a guy that put a curse on another guy once for cursing him out and this guy went around to say he was sorry. This was right near A.P. Hill, Virginia. Anyway, this guy went up to his door and knocked and the guy that put a curse on him came to the door and asked him what he wanted. Only he had this little smile on his face and when that guy went to tell him what he wanted, he couldn't say a mumbling word. No lie."

"I'd go down there myself," Leslie said.

"Catch this bad short," Kwami said, and they all looked up as a long sleek limousine pulled up in front of the house. It stopped and two men got out. They looked at a piece of paper and at the house numbers. Then one of them walked up to where the kids were sitting.

"Please to excuse us." The round little man had grey eyes and white eyebrows that seemed to fit perfectly with his thick accent. "Is dis Three Fifty-six Vest Vun Hundred and Tventy-second Street?"

Kitty looked at me and I looked at Leslie who looked at Judy. Finally we all shrugged. The two men, both of whom were dressed in black, looked up at the number over the door and then had a conference between themselves. Every once in a while they would look over to where we were sitting. Finally they both smiled and came back over to the stoop. This time they spoke to Judy.

"Excuse me, do you know a Mr. Villie Brown?"

"Who, me?"

"Da." They both nodded.

"I'm sorry, but I don't speak no English," Judy said.

Just then Willie looked out from his window and gave a hello.

"Villie?" The younger man smiled and waved. "Dere's Villie, now."

They both went down the four steps to Willie's house and disappeared inside. The long sleek limousine, a chauffeur still at the wheel, waited ominously by the curbside.

"Let's get out of here," Kwami said.

"Why?"

"I think that's the Mafia," Kwami answered.

"Heck, no, those are Russians." Judy said. "No lie."

"Come on up to my house," I said.

"Mama Doc! Where are you?"

The coal black cat lifted its head slowly and looked in the direction of Drusilla who was putting what was left of her package on the table. Drusilla poured some milk into a tin pie pan and put it under the sink. Mama Doc jumped easily down from her shelf and went to it, stopping halfway to put her front paws well in front of her and stretch.

"Stupid child almost knock me clear out of this world! I walking along, minding not a soul's business in this whole world but my own, and along comes this child like a bat out of a dark place and send me flying in the middle of the street.

"Don't you be catching airs at me, Mama Doc, I told you what happened. I would have been back here so long ago you wouldn't have missed me, wasn't for that long-headed fool. Why they make these children so foolish?"

Mama Doc looked up from her pan of milk and caught a white drop that dangled precariously on her whiskers with one quick flick of her tongue.

"If they ain't ripping and running down the street they got them radio and tape things stuck up to their ears and popping their fingers like nobody in the world ever heard of no music before except them. You know what, Mama Doc? Willie getting foolish just like them. Everytime I see that man he got some kind of new idea to make a lot of money or how he can take it easy. He better stay on that job he got. What you leaving that milk for, Mama Doc? If I take it up from there I sure ain't gonna put it back so you better finish it while you got the chance.

"Then this little long-headed boy got the nerve to say he sorry. He sorry. And all his little ugly friends standing around like they got a bellyful of giggles they can't keep in. I wish I could believe that little fool was meaning to hit me. You know what I'd do to him, Mama Doc? I'd put a fix on him so's everytime he'd see a bicycle it'd make him sick to his fool stomach . . . "

Two

My parents worked so no one was home when we got there. I took some cookies out of the closet (the Vanilla Wafers because I always saved the Fig Newtons for myself), and dumped them on a plate. I also broke out some cans of soda. I really wasn't worried about Drusilla or anything like that. Not worried like I would have been if I had really done something wrong, but still . . . there was no use in taking unnecessary chances.

I took everybody into my room because mom said that I had to when she wasn't home. Which was cool by me. She had fixed the room up nice so it looked more like a living room than a bedroom, and everybody dug it. I even had a fold-up Ping-Pong table in the room which, naturally, Kwami pulled down and started one of his imaginary games. He played more imaginary games than anybody I ever heard of.

"How come Willie is messin' with those Russians?" Leslie asked.

"I don't know," Anthony answered. No one had reached for the cookies yet, but Anthony had one hand resting on the table near the plate in case there was a general grab.

"Obviously you don't know," Kwami said, slamming an imaginary Ping-Pong ball past an imaginary opponent. "That's why we're up here—to figure out why the dude got a limousine in *front* of his shack, Russians *in* his shack, and an air of mystery lurking about his long head."

"I thought we were up here to see about how we were going to get Drusilla to leave Dean alone," Leslie said.

"That's because the mind of Leslie can only grasp 'local' issues while my mind struggles with the 'global' issues and the interplanetary happenings. This turkey's little skirmish with Drusilla Gorilla is minor league in the big ball game of L-I-F-E. Dig?"

"I don't really care about the Russians, or whatever they are," I said, watching Kwami take a handful of cookies. "I think we should take care of first things first since this is my house and my cookies." I pulled the plate just out of Kwami's reach. "Dig?"

"Logical, extremely logical, my good man." Kwami rubbed his chin. "Pass the cookies and we'll attend to your problem right away."

I passed the cookies and Kwami swept the remaining ones on the plate onto the Ping-Pong table.

"The way I see it, you should throw yourself on the mercy of the court," he continued. "Tell her that you're sorry and that you will rely upon her mercy."

"What good will that do if she's really mad?"

"It'll make her feel bad when she does your pitiful rump in, that's all. You are done for, my man. There's no power on earth that will save your soul from the clutches of Drusilla Gorilla. If I were you I'd just throw myself away. Your hour of doom is in the room. Your moment of fate is waitin' at the gate."

"I kind of agree with Kwami," said Anthony. "I mean, nothing personal and all that, but there's nothing you can do to get away from a Mojo lady, man. You done for, Jim."

"I don't even know what Mojo is," I said.

"That doesn't mean a thing," Kwami chimed in. "I knew a guy that didn't know a thing about Oldsmobiles until he got knocked down by one."

"Mojo is like magic," Leslie said. "Except it's used to get people to do things or to get even with them."

"I know it's like magic, but I still don't know if I

really believe in it," I said. "I remember in school we learned a little about Voodoo and the teacher said it only worked because some people believed in it. If a man said you were going to be sick and you believed it, you'd probably get sick. If you don't believe in it then you won't get sick. That makes a lot of sense to me."

"People don't believe in Mojo because they don't know anything about it. If your teacher knew more about it he might believe it," said Leslie. "Anyway, there's a lot of things people know is true today but didn't believe in before. If someone told me you could send pictures of people through the air from California into my living room, I wouldn't believe it. But then there's the old television sitting there with its own Mojo working."

"The trouble is I do believe in Mojo a little," I said. "There are so many things that I don't understand exactly but that seem as if they ought to be true. Some people *are* different. I don't know if Drusilla can really do Mojo or anything but she's sure different. And look how mad she got when she wasn't even hurt."

I opened a soda, took a sip, and put it on the mantel.

"Some people get mad and say a lot of things but then they forget them," Judy added.

"If she's going to do something to me I hope she doesn't tell me," I said. "On the other hand, I sure would like to know what she's thinking about."

"I still think you're done for," Anthony repeated.

"I don't think he's done for." Leslie was talking with her mouth full. "I had an aunt once who was born with a veil over her eyes and she knew Mojo and she taught me some of it. I think I can get her spell off of you."

"The battle of the hexes." Kwami stood up and waved his fingers at me. "And you're the booby-prize."

"I'm serious. All you have to do is to make sure that she can't get anything that grows on you."

"You mean like the fungus in his ears?"

"Kwami, you better shut up and be serious. Dean is *supposed* to be your friend."

"That's why I want to stay away from him," Kwami said. "I know that he wouldn't want his last thought, as he is slipping away into that Great Beyond—"

"In the shape of a one-eyed frog—" added Judy.

"—in the shape of a one-eyed frog, that his best friend was also being wasted. I mean, if we all get wasted who's gonna sit around and say all them cool things about you, man?"

"Yeah." Anthony wiped some crumbs from his mouth. "Like, 'Hey, remember Dean, wasn't he a good old guy before he hit the Mojo mamma from Manhattan?' "

"Dean, you were a nice guy, all kidding aside," said Kitty.

"Come on, I'm not gone yet. You people make me feel awful, man! Well, anyway, I'm going over there," I said.

"Over where?" Judy asked.

"To Drusilla's house."

"To Drusilla's house?" Anthony's eyes widened.

"I might as well be brave about it. No use wondering what she's going to do. I'll just go over and ask her."

"Well, my man, all I have to say is good-bye," Kwami said. "It's been nice knowing you."

"Kwami, why don't you keep quiet," Judy said. "Having you for a friend is like having a bad case of poison ivy Everybody knows you're around but you don't do a bit of good."

"Why don't you just shut up before I give you a fat lip?" Kwami stood up.

"Which one, your top one or your bottom one?"

"There goes the limousine!" I looked out of the window just in time to see the limousine pull away from the curb and turn toward Morningside Avenue. "And here comes Willie out of the basement, too."

"Put out the light in case he looks up here," Leslie said.

Judy put out the light. We watched Willie walk to the corner and turn toward Milbank Center.

"There's something going on," Kitty said, shaking her head.

Judy put the light back on.

"Look, let's solve one problem at a time," I said. "First, let's solve my problem with Drusilla and then we'll worry about Willie, okay?"

"When are you going over there?" Kwami asked. "I'll go with you."

"Right now," I answered.

"Right now?" Kwami looked at me and then over to the others.

"Yeah, but don't worry," I said. "I'll go over by myself. I think she lives across from the projects. I saw her and Willie go into a place over there and I saw her sitting at a window once."

I don't even know why I said I was going over to Drusilla's house. The more I thought about it the worse the idea seemed to be. Anyway, I had said it, and before I knew it I was on my way. I took the long route, up a Hundred and Twenty-third Street past the school and then down Amsterdam Avenue. When I got to the building I started to go right in, and then I saw how gloomy it looked. I walked past once or twice, trying to see down the hall but I couldn't. I wished I had waited for Kwami. I took a deep breath, wet my lips a little, and went in.

Some of the mailboxes were broken, and only a few of them had names printed on them or just above them on the wall. The boxes all had numbers on them and I looked for the ones beginning with the number one, since I thought I had seen Drusilla looking out of a front first-floor window. There were four apartments beginning with one, 1-A, 1-B, 1-C and 1-D. Apartment 1-A had the name Martinez printed on it, and the one marked 1-C had the name Pedro Jones above it. The other two boxes did not have names on them and I figured one of them had to be Drusilla's.

The first apartment I got to was 1-B. I figured that

must have been Drusilla's apartment because it was right across from 1-A, and one of the first two apartments had to be hers because she lived in the front. Still, I figured I might as well check out the back apartment first. I went to 1-D and knocked on the door.

A Spanish lady opened the door and asked what I wanted. Before I could open my mouth she slammed the door shut. Maybe the whole house was filled with weirdos, I thought.

The door to apartment 1-B was covered with tin that had been painted red. On all four corners of the door there were pictures of little people. They were almost like a child's drawings, only children don't draw little people on the corners of somebody's door in dark hallways. This had to be Drusilla's place, I thought. I felt a knot in the pit of my stomach. I was really scared. I don't even know why I was scared but I was. Then I remembered what those zombies looked like on television and I remembered why.

I was standing there thinking and scrinching down at the same time. I was trying to think about what I was going to say to Drusilla when she opened the door. "Why, good afternoon, Drusilla. I do hope you're feeling well." Maybe something like that. Also, I was scrinching down because I'm tall for my age. When I was eleven, the women in the booths at the movies started giving me funny looks when I told them how old I was. Anyway, if you're tall people always give you a hard time. If you're short they give you a break.

Well, I was standing there thinking and scrinching down when the Spanish lady down the hall opened her door and slammed it shut again. I figured she must have thought I was a mugger or something. So I reached up and knocked on Drusilla's door.

At first I didn't hear anything and I figured that maybe she wasn't home. Then I heard a little noise but the door still didn't open. I figured I'd count to ten and then split. I wasn't going to knock on the door again and that's for sure. I got to five before I heard this voice call out from the apartment.

"Who there?"

"It's me," I said. "I'm a friend of Willie's." I hadn't even meant to add that but it sure sounded good.

The door opened without a sound and I nearly jumped out of my skin. Drusilla was standing in front of the door. She was wearing a long grey robe that came down to her ankles. There was a light coming from the apartment that made her hair look like thousands of spiderwebs piled crazily on top of each other.

"You the devil that tried to kill me, ain't you? *Ain't you?*"

"Yes, ma'am." I didn't want to say exactly that but that's what came out.

"Come on in here."

She reached out with one of her skinny arms and took me by the shoulder.

I was in the apartment almost before I realized it. She clicked two locks on the door behind me and then pointed toward a chair in front of the table. I was kind of glad that it was near the door but the way my feet felt, as if they were three times as heavy as normal, I didn't think I'd be doing anything that took a lot of speed.

There was a strange smell in Drusilla's apartment. I was pretty sure it was incense but I wasn't positive. On the sink there were three candles which were lit. A roach scurried along the wall and went into an opening in a box of soap powder. It was funny thinking about a Mojo lady having roaches in her apartment until I thought that she probably *wanted* to have roaches in her apartment.

"Willie send you here?"

I looked away from where the roach had gone into the soap powder right into Drusilla's eyes. I shook my head no, that he hadn't, and she asked me why I had come.

"I just wanted to tell you that I was sorry for, you know, hitting you with my bicycle and all and wondered if you would. . . . " I ran out of words right in the middle of the sentence. I wasn't going to ask her not to put a Mojo on me, that's for sure. She might have forgotten all about it and me asking her not to do it might just remind her to do it. In fact, the more I thought about it, just me coming past her house might have reminded her of the whole thing.

"What's the matter with you, boy, some cat got your tongue?"

I couldn't help wondering if she had a cat. I was trying to think of something else to say when there was a low whistling noise and Drusilla got up and went to the stove. There were two pots on the stove, one was one of those teapots that whistled when the water boiled and the other was just a regular pot. Drusilla turned off the teapot and got two cups from the closet. She put the cups on the table, one in front of me and one where she had been sitting. Then she got what looked like the bark of a tree, only a little reddish, and put a little in each cup and poured hot water over it.

"Have some tea," she said. "It's good for what's wrong with you."

There wasn't nothing wrong with me. I didn't know why she had to give me something to fix me up if there wasn't anything wrong with me in the first place. Unless she did something to me that I didn't know about. If she thought I was going to drink that spooky-behind tea she had another think coming to her.

Anyway, I'm staring down at the tea when I hear this tearing noise. I looked up and there's Drusilla looking like I don't know what and tearing this photograph up. First she tore it into two pieces, and then she tore them in half, and then she tore the little pieces into even smaller pieces. Then she took all the pieces and dropped them into the other pot.

Now if she had thrown them away it would have been cool. Or if she had said some words over them or something like that it would have been all right, too. But when she dropped them into a pot and started cooking them I felt like my stomach was just about to fall down through my feet. I looked down again 'cause I didn't even want to see what she was doing next.

She went into her pocket and pulled out an envelope. Inside the envelope there was some short hair, like you see laying around the floor in a barbershop. Drusilla put it in the palm of her hand and pushed it around with one finger until it was all in the middle of her palm.

"What are you doing?" I asked.

"My cousin got her a no 'count man what done up and gone heself and she big as a house with the devil's child. I make he so weak he can't stand tall enough to spit on another woman."

She put the hair in a bowl and, taking a bottle from a cabinet beneath the sink, poured what smelled like vinegar over it. Then she took the mixture and poured it into the pot with the photograph.

"Where is he now?" I asked.

"She think he in Shreveport," Drusilla answered. "Why you don't like the tea?"

"Oh, I like it, but I really can't stay very long," I said. "I just thought I would stop by and say hello and everything."

Drusilla came back to the table and looked at me over the edge of the teacup as she drank. The room wasn't very bright to begin with, and the steam rising in wisps from the cup made Drusilla's face look as if it were fading in and out. I picked up the teacup and placed it in front of my mouth. I lifted the edge and pretended to drink. The tea was very hot and didn't smell like any tea I ever drank before.

"What are those signs for, on the door?"

"To keep the dead away," Drusilla answered, her eyes never leaving me

"Oh." I could picture the souls of dead people standing outside of Drusilla's door waiting to get in. I wondered why they wanted to get in but was too afraid of what the answer might be to ask. "I guess you can do just about anything, huh?"

Drusilla smiled and I saw that one of her front teeth was made of gold.

"I don't know what I'm going to do with you, yet," Drusilla said. "You almost kill me with that bicycle, child."

I took a deep breath and held it. The thing I wanted to do most, besides getting away from Drusilla, was to go to the bathroom.

"I think I'd better be going." Drusilla didn't say anything. I backed toward the door and fumbled with the locks for a while before it opened. I looked over at Drusilla. She was still sitting there looking at me. I couldn't tell if she was smiling or not. I closed the door quietly and started walking slowly down the hallway, trying to remain calm. Then I thought of the signs on

Drusilla's door that kept the dead people out and took off running. I ran all the way back to One Hundred and Twenty-second Street and into the house.

"Well, what you think of that, Mama Doc? You ever see such big eyes in all your natural born life? I thought they were gonna pop right out his head. First he looking in the corners, then he looking over at the sink. First I didn't even hear him, he knock so timid. Tapping like he afraid the door gonna hit him back, or something.

"You need a bath, Mama Doc. And don't go looking like you don't want one 'cause you're gonna get one if you want it or not. I ain't gonna have you around here smelling like no alley cat.

"I'm glad he came over. My head's pounding like I don't know what. That Willie is the most troublesome man I ever did see. I don't know what's the matter with him. He come calling me up the other day saying he wants me to meet some white people, like I ain't never met no white people before—that was the day I brought you them chicken livers from the meat market. Anyway, he come saying he wants me to meet these white people. I know he's up to something because it's baby this and baby that when he wants me to do something for him. That's a sure sign, Mama Doc.

"I was doing something for my cousin down home and I couldn't even concentrate on what I was doing until that boy came in here. What did he say his name was? I don't think he ever did say what his name was. Oh, he was scared all right. Guess he done heard those stories about me being a witch and whatever. You should have jumped off your shelf and landed on his back. Child, his eyes would have run in one direction and his feet would in another! This stew ain't gonna be worth two cents, Mama Doc, not two cents."

Drusilla sniffed the contents of a large pot and then tasted it. She made a face and added a quarter of a bay leaf and some thyme. She stirred it again with a wooden spoon.

"You know, half the people in this part of the country is scared of cats. Yes they are, too. 'Specially a black cat. If you walked down the street in front of people you'd have them dancin' all over the sidewalk, trying to get out of your way. Well, that's the way it goes. People who don't know nothing are afraid of everything. People who know something at least know what to be afraid of. That little bicycle boy, just look at him. Did you see him, Mama Doc? He was afraid of me. He didn't do nothing what you would call terrible but child, was he afraid! Took my mind off Willie, anyway. Mama Doc, what you think these people be wanting with me and Willie?"

Three

The next day I told the group the entire story.

"You mean she was cooking this cat's picture with some hair and that was going to mess him up clear down in Shreveport?" Kwami asked for the third time.

"I don't think we better mess with her," Wayne said. "I don't think we ought to mess with nobody ever again."

"What we have to do," Judy said, "is get Willie to

35

talk to her. Willie seems like a nice guy."

"He'd better be," Kwami said, "or Drusilla Gorilla will pop his Polaroid into the pot and there will be an Instamatic disaster."

"But if we can get something on him," I said. "Then maybe we can get him to do something about Drusilla."

"You mean blackmail?" Leslie asked.

"You can't blackmail black people," Kwami said. "We're going to have to whitemail him."

"We don't even know if he's doing something wrong," Wayne said.

"Then how come he's hanging around those Russians?" I asked.

"That's right," Leslie said. "He wouldn't be hanging around for nothing."

"That's not right at all," Judy nearly shouted. "Just because people do things that you don't expect them to be doing, it doesn't mean that they're doing somethin' wrong. I don't know why people always say things like that."

I knew Judy was saying that mainly because she had had a big fight with her parents about hanging out in a black neighborhood. They had wanted to send her away to one of those camps where you learn to play tennis for the summer but she didn't want to go.

"Well let's check him out because he might be a spy," Kitty said. "I ain't never checked out no spy before."

"Willie is a porter, case closed," Kwami said. "The only thing that Willie can sell the Russians is garbage."

"Maybe," I said, "that's all they're interested in. Maybe they can figure out something from the garbage. Let's face it, they're not hanging around for nothing. And Willie is always getting into something. Remember that time he got into that thing where he was gonna have all of us swim the English Channel at one time?"

"Yeah, he was going to get us all in the newspapers at one time and then we were going to get on the quiz shows and make a lot of money or something."

There was a chorus of rights.

"So getting involved in something isn't unusual for Willie. But maybe he doesn't know what he's involved in this time. He may not think he's doing something wrong, but—"

"Hey, man, he's still a porter."

"Okay, what would you rather have if you were a Russian spy—top secret garbage or everything that Kwami knows?"

"Hey, that's right," Judy said. "Willie might be giving them information without even knowing about it. If we can find out what's going on we can use that to get Willie to make Drusilla leave Dean alone."

"Why don't we just call up the FBI?"

"Because if we're wrong," Kwami said, "and the FBI comes down on Willie and Willie is clean, then he's going to be mad."

"And if Willie gets mad, Drusilla will be mad," added Wayne.

"And if Drusilla gets mad, Dean is in trouble."

"Let's find out if they're really Russians first," Kwami said. "About a year ago some guys with accents came around looking for Bunky Johnson's mother and they were just from the finance company. My mind is really working in top gear now so don't interrupt me."

"His mouth is working pretty good, too," Judy threw in.

"Ignore the ravings of that poor unfortunate creature," Kwami said, "and get on with your plan. First you have to have a code name for the operation."

"How come?" asked Kitty.

"Because the walls have ears, baby. You don't know who's a spy and who's not a spy these days. That's why. Anyway, that's the way they do it in the movies. The code word for this operation will be Brother Bad."

"What's that mean?" I asked.

"Nothing. That's why it's so bad, brother."

"Hey, that's cool."

"I'm hip," Kwami said, giving himself five. "Now, the first thing we have to do is to identify the enemy. We got to find out if them cats are really Russians. That will be Anthony, Judy, and Kitty 's job. They will follow these cats the next time they show up and see where they go. If they go to some place that looks like Moscow, we know we got them."

"How we going to follow them when they have a car?" asked Kitty.

"We could take the subway," Anthony volunteered.

"Right, and then get off at every stop and ask everybody if they've seen two Russians drive by, right?"

"You know what we could do," Judy said, "we could follow them as far as we could and see where they go, right? Then the next time they come around one of us could go there and start following from there until we couldn't follow them anymore and then we'd know where they went."

"Or we could ask around and see where all the Russians hung out."

"That's cool except they might not be Russians."

"That brings me to part two of my plan," Kwami said. "Me and Dean and Leslie will sneak into Willie's place and look around. See if he's got any secret stuff in the basement."

"Sometimes spies have false bottoms in their closets with secret transmitters and stuff in them," said Anthony.

"How about Drusilla?" I asked.

"Okay, I forgot about Drusilla. Leslie will keep an eye out for her and report any strange happenings. And tomorrow we'll start the first phase of Operation Brother Bad by investigating the residence of one Long Willie."

Four

The first day of Operation Brother Bad was a disaster. We met in the park as arranged. Anthony brought Wayne along and there was a meeting to decide whether or not he should be included in the operation. It was decided that he would be. It was also decided that everyone had to be sworn to secrecy. Wayne said that he couldn't swear unless he had his mother's permission, but me and Kwami threw him down on the ground and made him swear anyway and told him that if he revealed any of the secrets we would personally drop him down a sewer. The one thing Wayne feared more than anything else in the world was rats, and he knew that the sewers were filled with them. After everyone was sworn in, Judy and the transportation group— the one who were going to follow the men in the limousine—parked at the corner with their bicycles and waited for the limousine to show up. Kwami and me went down in the basement with Wayne behind us and Leslie sitting on the stoop as a lookout.

The rain started to pour about eleven o'clock. We found out later that the transportation squad had tried to huddle their bikes against the side of the building but it was no use. They were getting drenched. Judy started sneezing and so did Kitty. Anthony said he saw his mother coming down the street and that she had signaled for him to come home. Judy and Kitty said that they didn't see his mother but Anthony left anyway.

Meanwhile Leslie left, too. So there wasn't any lookout for Kwami and me and Wayne.

Kwami went in first. Wayne followed and I brought up the rear. Willie lived in an apartment that began just past the boiler room. We had all been to Willie's place from time to time listening to his stories about how great a basketball player he used to be and how he almost got a scholarship to U.C.L.A.

"I think I heard something," Wayne said in this real loud whisper.

"Come on, Wayne, you're always hearing things," I said. Wayne was really scary and would run at the drop of a hat. He was okay, though. The funny thing about him was that he looked just like his father. I mean just like his father only a little younger. I figured his father must have been scary, too.

The further we went down the hall toward where Willie lived, the darker it got. There was a light bulb somewhere that Willie used to screw into a wall socket to turn on.

"Turn on the light," Wayne whispered. It sounded like a good idea to me.

"Can't," Kwami whispered back. "If we turn on the light, they'll know we were here. This way, if we get the signal that someone is coming we can just run out and they won't suspect anything."

By the time we reached the boiler room door we were all getting pretty nervous. Kwami gave the door a push and nothing happened. Wayne wanted to leave and I was just about ready to agree with him.

"It's not locked, it's just heavy, that's all," Kwami said, putting his shoulder against the door. "Come on, give me a hand."

I began to help Kwami push the door open when all of a sudden Wayne began to cry.

"Turn the light on, quick," he said. "There's something on my neck."

"Come on, man," I said, "it's spooky enough down here without you—"

"Please . . . pleeease." Wayne was really sniffing now and I knew that in another minute he'd really be crying.

"Yeah," Kwami said. You could tell he was really disgusted with Wayne. He slid his hand along the wall until he found the light fixture and then screwed in the bulb. At first the light hurt our eyes and and we couldn't see anything. Then I looked at Wayne and saw it. Sitting right on his neck, its antennas waving back and forth and everything, was the biggest waterbug I had ever seen in my life.

I turned toward Kwami and by the look on his face I knew he had seen it, too. I jumped back a little and Kwami jumped back, and then Wayne let out a scream you wouldn't believe. He tried to knock the roach off and all I could think of was I didn't want him to knock it off on me. He finally got it and knocked it toward Kwami who knocked it right back toward him. When it came back toward Wayne he fell backward trying to get out of the way and it landed on his chest. Kwami saw an old broom leaning against the wall and grabbed it to hit the waterbug with but just knocked out the light instead. When he did that I took off, and I could hear Kwami coming right behind me. We got out of the basement and out into the street in about no time. It was pouring and there was no sign of Leslie. Kitty came up on her bike and told us that Willie was coming. She was soaking wet.

Me and Kwami ran down to Manhattan Avenue to

Kwami's house and I almost got hit by a car as we were crossing the street. We ran up the two flights to his apartment and got there just as his father, who was a truck driver for the post office, was leaving to go to work.

"What's it doing, raining outside?" Kwami's father asked. He could see that we were wet, but he always asked questions like that.

Kwami shook his head that it was raining.

"You boys were running, eh?" was the answer.

"Yeah." Kwami panted. I was leaning against the wall trying not to throw up. My lunch was bouncing around in my chest and I didn't think I was going to hold it much longer. Finally Kwami's father went on downstairs, and we went in and laid on the floor in Kwami's room.

"Hey, man, did you see that waterbug on Wayne's neck?"

"That was the biggest waterbug I ever saw in my life," I said. "That sucker must have been three inches long."

"That was a Japanese vampire roach." Kwami was still having trouble getting his breath. "I saw them once on television. Channel Seven."

"You think Willie had anything to do with them?" I asked.

"No, they just trying to take over the world on their own."

The doorbell rang and it was Wayne, standing in the hallway crying and wet.

"You gonna let him in?"

"Hey, Wayne, that roach still on you?" Kwami called out through the peephole.

"No, open the door."

"You sure?"

"Yeah, it fell off. Open the door, I'm bleeding."

"What happened?"

"Open the door."

"If that vampire roach sucked his blood, he may be under their power. Does he look roachy?"

"I don't know. You take a look."

I looked through the peephole at Wayne. He was still crying and the tears had smudged their way through the grime on his cheeks. He stood back and held up his leg. The pants were torn at the knee and he was bleeding, but not really enough to get excited about. Kwami made him turn around twice and checked him to make sure that the waterbug wasn't still on him before he let him in.

"You guys are rotten, man," Wayne was whining. He had stopped crying in the hallway but the tears started all over again.

"You were the one that was afraid of the roach," I said.

"That wasn't no roach, that was a waterbug," Wayne said. "And you two guys were the first to run."

"Did you see Willie when you got outside?" Kwami asked.

"No, but those Russians were just pulling up when I hit the sidewalk."

"I think we're gonna have to get us a new plan," Kwami said.

I figured that it was just about time for Kwami to say something like that. Plans are cool as long as they work, but as soon as a few things start going wrong everybody wants to do something else. What I wanted to do was to go back to dealing with Drusilla. I kept thinking about the guy in the photograph down in Louisiana and the pot of boiling water and the vinegar and all. Wayne started talking about how was he going to explain the tear in his pants to his mother and Kwami wanted to switch everything off on the Russians. I didn't know what Willie was doing fooling around with the Russians but that wasn't really my problem. I had two problems. One, I wanted to find out about that guy in Louisiana. I wondered if he was all right or whether he was wasted. I could just imagine him sitting around when she dropped his picture with the vinegar and hair and stuff into that pot. He probably didn't feel good all of a sudden. He might have died.

The second problem I had was to find out exactly how mad Drusilla was at me. The way she just looked at me when I left made my blood run cold. I didn't even like to say things like "make my blood run cold" or to think it, just in case she did it. I told Kwami and Wayne that

I wanted to deal with the first problem and told them that if they were really mature that's what they would do. What we ended up doing was calling everybody up and arranging for a meeting for the next day at three in the afternoon.

We had to call the meeting for that time because Kwami had to go downtown with his mother in the morning to buy shoes.

This time we met behind the church. Judy, Kitty, Leslie, Wayne, Anthony and I were already there when Kwami arrived. Also present was Major, Judy's white terrier.

"How come you brought that mutt along? We don't need any dogs around to complicate things." Kwami stuck his fist into Major's face and Major licked it happily.

"I brought the dog for a reason," Judy said, pulling the small dog closer to her and rubbing him behind the neck. "Now why don't you go on and call the meeting to order."

"Yeah, okay." Kwami stood up and looked around to make sure there were no outsiders. "The third meeting of Operation Brother Bad is now in session. Anybody got anything to report?"

"Yeah, me." Judy waved her hand.

"You always have something to say."

"Well, when those Russians came around I tried to follow them but they got away too quick in that fancy car they got. Anyway, I got the license plate number, and me and Kitty looked in the telephone book and found out where the Russian Embassy was and we rode over there and looked around but we didn't see nothing. So then we looked in the telephone book again and saw a place where they ate, a tea room or something over near Fifty-seventh Street, and we rode over there, too."

"Still didn't see the car, so we figured that maybe they changed cars every day," Kitty added.

"Or at least changed license plates," Judy continued. "But then we figured that since those buggers were always going uptown and we were looking downtown that we'd look in the Bronx telephone book."

"And that's where they had a listing for the Russian Consulate and so we went all the way up to a place called Riverdale." Kitty nodded her head. "And we only made one stop."

"It wasn't so bad after we got past One Hundred and Fifty-fifth Street because the hills weren't so bad. We stopped at White Tower . . . "

"And had some of those little hamburgers they sell . . . "

"Will you people get on with it? What did you find out?" Kwami was a little put out that Kitty and Judy had obviously found something and were drawing it out.

"We found the limousine right in front of the Russian Consulate building."

"They're definitely Russians, and Willie is definitely a spy!" Judy said. "I think we should turn him over to the FBI."

"Not until we take care of Drusilla. Maybe we—" I started to protest.

"We thought about that already, too," Kitty said. "That's why Judy brought Major along. Leslie's gonna try out her Mojo on Major, and if it works on him then she's gonna put a reverse fix on Dean so anybody else who tries to fix him gets fixed themselves."

"Right, and once you put a reverse fix on somebody they can't ever get fixed again as long as they live," Leslie said, rummaging around in a large embroidered bag she had brought along.

"You really gonna fix that dog?" Kwami asked.

"Yep."

"How you gonna fix him?" asked Kwami. "I mean what are you going to turn him into?"

"I'm going to give him the mind of a sparrow," Leslie answered. She had taken a piece of chalk out of the bag and knelt down and drew a circle on the ground about the size of a basketball. "See if he'll fit into that circle."

Judy tried to get Major to sit in the circle. She picked him up and put him in the middle of it twice but he kept scampering away. Finally she got him to sit still by standing very close to him, almost touching the edge of the circle with her foot. When Major sat in the circle he just about fit. All except his tail, of course, which wagged over the edge of the circle. Leslie drew a bigger circle around him and he fit perfectly, even when he lay down with his head on his paws. Then she drew four stars around the circle.

"How are you going to know when he's got the mind of a sparrow?" Kitty asked.

"When he starts looking like Wayne," Anthony said.

"If it's a sparrow's brain, it's got to be Wayne!" Kwami gave himself five.

Wayne started to protest.

"How can you tell?" Kitty asked again.

" 'Cause he'll try to fly toward the moon," Leslie answered.

"Fly toward what moon? You sure you haven't got yourself a little too deep in your Mojo, mama?" Kwami closed one eye and leaned back a little.

"We're not doing it now, we have to do it at midnight," Leslie said. "We all have to come back here at the stroke of midnight. That's the best time to do anything like this." Leslie drew another circle and measured it to see if it would be the same size as the first one. It was. "It would be even better if we could do it in a graveyard."

"No way," Wayne started backing up. "I ain't going in no graveyard."

"Don't be ridiculous, Wayne," Anthony said. "There aren't any graveyards in the city, man. If you die they got to take you out to Long Island or Jersey to bury you."

"Wait a minute." Kwami scratched his chin. "Ain't no way my mother is gonna let me hustle out of the house at no stroke of no midnight. The only people in the world who would be out at that time of night are you Mojo people."

"And muggers," Kitty added.

"Well, as long as we can get out after dark so we can tell where the moon is."

"I don't think I can come out after dark," Wayne said. "My mother don't like to be in the house by herself."

"I'll be here," Kitty shrugged.

"Well, it oughtta be dark about seven," Judy said. "Me and Major'll be here."

"Yeah, I guess I'll be here, too," Kwami said. "And you better be here, Dean, or I'll get Leslie to put a magnifying Mojo on you so whatever Drusilla does will go double. Instead of speaking with a forked tongue, it'll be split four ways and you'll be talking in quadraphonic sound."

"I'll be here."

"Me, too," Anthony said.

"You gonna show up, Wayne? If you don't you can't be part of the operation anymore. We're all gonna meet right here at exactly seven o'clock."

Five

⊂⊫ Wayne showed up with Leslie. Everyone was there by five minutes past seven, with Judy and Major being the last to show.

"My mother asked me where I was going and I said I had to fix something," Judy said.

"Hey, that's cool," Leslie laughed. "Her mother asked her where she—"

"I heard her," Kwami said. "Now let's get on with this thing before it gets too dark."

"I think Kwami is afraid of the dark," Judy said.

"You don't be playing with Mojo." Leslie's voice seemed kind of strange and Wayne jumped a little.

"I was just kidding, no lie," Judy found herself whispering.

"Put the subject in the circle." Leslie was still speaking in the strange voice. Judy sat Major in the middle of the circle and held him by the collar as he licked her hand. Then Leslie stood and took three steps backward from the circle, turned and took a candle from her pocket, lit it and placed it on the ground. Then she went back to the circle and backed off three steps in a different direction and lit a second candle. None of us spoke as she lit a third candle three steps in yet another direction.

Then she went into her bag and pulled out a plastic bag which contained a bloody object.

"Hey, Leslie, what's in that bag?" Kwami took a step backward. "I ain't playing nothing too funny, now."

"There is the heart and liver of a freshly killed chicken." Leslie's voice was dry on the night air.

"You didn't have all that stuff this afternoon," Anthony said.

"It wasn't defrosted this afternoon "

"Man, we ought to let Dean stay here by himself," Wayne said. "We ain't really that good friends."

I didn't answer that one.

"Out of the black night of death came the evil spirits of the tormented dead," Leslie began. "They will do the bidding of she who holds the sacrifice of blood within the candle altar. They will do the bidding of she who holds the flesh of cruel and bloody death within the candle altar. Out of the black night of death this blood will spill upon the victim."

Leslie poured some of the blood from the plastic bag into the circle.

"Now they will do the bidding of she who holds the flesh of cruel and bloody death within the candle altar. This is my bidding. Give the victim the mind of the bird that flies in winter snow and tempest strong. Give the victim the mind of the sparrow." Leslie raised the heart and liver high above her head.

"When this flesh falls within the circle it will be done."

About this time I had just about had enough of this whole thing. When you talk about Mojo and stuff like that, or voodoo, it's all right with me. Especially when you talk about it in the daytime in school with all the lights on and early enough so that you can forget it by the time you go to bed. But when you start fooling around with real blood, from something that was really living at one time, in the middle of the night, then that's just a little too much.

It got colder and colder as we listened to Leslie. The trees, just ordinary in the daytime, suddenly got too spooky, and the wind started picking up leaves and blowing them around.

When Leslie dropped the raw flesh into the circle next

to Major none of us made a sound. Major whined a little and tried to get out of the circle and go to Judy, but she just pushed him back in. He turned back toward the raw meat and sniffed it carefully. I looked up at Leslie and she was staring at Major with this weird look. Suddenly Major barked once, then again, and then began to eat the liver.

"Hey, is he supposed to eat the Mojo?" Kwami asked.

"I don't think so . . . " Leslie tried to push Major away from the meat with her foot.

Wayne fell to one knee and put his arms around the dog and tried to pull him away.

"Don't get in the circle or the fix will be on you!" Leslie gave Wayne a shove away from the magic circle and he fell over backwards. As he did he released Major and the dog started running, knocking over one of the candles. Judy started running after him as fast as she could and I ran after her. I'm not exactly sure why but it seemed like a good idea at the time.

By the time Judy had caught up with Major, all of the liver was gone. He was scampering around Judy's legs as happy as he could be. Judy slipped his leash on him and we went back to where the rest of the group was standing around. Kwami, as usual, was running his mouth when we got there.

"I guess your Mojo didn't work too good."

"I can't help it if that dumb dog ate the bloody victim," Leslie said defensively.

"Where'd you get that 'victim' anyway?"

"From the supermarket," Leslie said.

"Listen. We're going to have to accelerate Operation Brother Bad a little, I guess, or my man Dean is doomed," said Anthony.

"Drusilla probably can't do it either," I said.

"Man, you're overlooking the obvious," Kwami said. "I mean if the day ain't here there ain't no sun, and if Drusilla can't do it it can't be done. Your days are numbered."

"I don't think you have anything to worry about for a while, though," Leslie said, "because they mostly do their fixing and things like that on nights with a full moon and on the stroke of midnight."

"That's probably why it didn't work on Major," said Wayne.

"And it won't be a full moon for at least until next week."

"Next week?" Kwami jumped in front of Leslie. "Did you say next week?"

"Kwami, stop acting crazy," Kitty said.

"Dean, you are in big trouble." Kwami pointed his finger at me. "Not only are your days numbered, but they are numbered in the units column. You are almost a used-to-be."

"A used-to-be?"

"Yeah, you used-to-be-Dean but now you going to be a frog or a rock or whatever else she going to turn you into. You in a world of trouble, boy. I wouldn't want to be in your sneakers for nothing in the world. OOOO----weeeee!! Good googla-moogla."

"Don't worry, Dean." Kitty took my hand in hers. "We just have to speed up the rest of the operation and get things settled sooner. I still don't think it's anything to get shook up about."

A funny thing happened when Kitty said that. Well, actually, it wasn't so much what she was saying but that she was holding my hand when she said it. I really liked it. For a moment I forgot all about the Mojo and Drusilla. It didn't last long though, because Kitty started talking to Judy and let go my hand.

"Let's have another meeting tomorrow, and we can decide exactly what we're going to do," Kwami said.

"Did you dudes find out anything when you got into Willie's place?" Leslie asked.

"We didn't even get into Willie's place."

"Oh, that's right," Judy laughed. "You were all too busy fighting a cockroach."

"That must have been some bad cockroach."

"Yeah, he must have known karate." Kitty helped Leslie carry the candles. "Can you imagine, three guys get scared away by one, count 'em, one cockroach. Embarrassing . . . "

"Wayne was the only one that was fighting the roach," Kwami said.

"That's because you and Dean split."

"You wouldn't have to worry about a roach." Kwami

turned toward Kitty. "As ugly as you are you'd of scared the roach more than he scared you."

"Shut up, Kwami, your I.Q. is hanging out again. See you people tomorrow."

"Just let me sit here and hold you for a while, Mama Doc, because the way I feel now I could just cry. I could just cry!"

Mama Doc purred contentedly as Drusilla gently stroked the back of her neck.

"You know what Willie wants me to do? Well, I'm gonna tell you. You remember them white people he said he wanted me to meet? Well, that's where I went today after work. That's why I left out your food because I knew I was gonna be late. I hope you didn't eat them up this morning like a pig.

"Anyway, I get the Number One-Oh-Four bus like Willie tells me and I get off at a Hundred and Third Street, see? Mind you I ain't never been on nobody's a Hundred Third Street and Broadway before, but I go on up there.

"Here comes Willie popping out of this long limousine like he's a jack in the box or something and his teeth all shining and whatnot. 'Hi, baby,' that's what he says to me. 'Hi, baby, I wants you to meet some friends of mine.'

" 'Where are they?' I ask.

⊂⊃ *58*

" 'They in the car,' says he.

" 'Well, let them get on out the car if they wants to meet me,' I said. I don't be getting in nobody's ve-hickle unless I know them first. You be getting into people's cars and they call you a loose woman. Well, Willie says come on and get into the car and I says I ain't doing nothing like that and he might as well not fix his mouth to say it again. So they get out and they come up to me and they start talking about how they heard I had some very interesting powers. I don't know what they talking about, Mama Doc, honest I don't. Well, they hemming and hawing and clearing their throats and talking round this and round that until all of a sudden I know what they talking about. They want me to explain what Mojo was. They got to be crazy and Willie got to be even more crazy. They don't know what they foolin' with. You don't go around explaining no Mojo. Why they want to know anyway? It won't do them no good.

"I was born with a veil over my eyes and a Mojo hand. What they gonna do, go back and get born again with a veil and a Mojo hand? Mama Doc, the fools they got in this world is something else, you hear? You ought to be a person, you wouldn't be no fool. I just got right back on that Number One-Oh-Four bus and went on back downtown 'til I got here. Now I got to go over and talk to Willie. He's supposed to know better than to be acting like that. He was running around those white people like I don't know what. Willie just got to know better than that.

"Mama Doc, there are some things in this people's world that you play with and some things that you don't play with. There are things going on, dark things, that people don't know about and maybe shouldn't know about. You know the kinds of things I'm talking about. Don't you? Don't you? I bet you just do, too."

Six

☰ "The logical thing to do is to let the Russians peep that we have peeped," Kwami said. "Then when they have peeped that we have peeped then they're gonna have to get their act together, dig?"

"Uh-uh." Judy shook her head.

"How come white people don't understand when you talk sense to them?" Kwami asked. He was doing some imaginary dribbling behind his back.

"I guess I must be part white because I don't understand either," Leslie said.

"Look, the whole reason that they can go around spying on people is what?" Kwami looked at us.

"They're Russians?" Wayne volunteered.

"No, dummy." Kwami shot an imaginary basketball right into Wayne's face. "Because no one knows what they're doing. Now if they know that we know what they're doing they have to stop, dig?"

"Either that or get rid of us," said Anthony. He pointed his finger at Kwami as if it were a gun. "I heard the Russians got this new gun that kills you so fast you can walk around the rest of your life without even knowing that you're dead."

"We don't let them know that it's us that knows, dig?" Kwami said. "We let them know that somebody knows but who knows they don't know. In other words we let them peep that somebody knows but we don't let them peep who it is."

"I think I understand," Judy said.

"Glory be." Kwami stood up and bowed elaborately. "It must be the dawning of a new day."

"They peep that their peeping is peeped but they don't know who is peeping their peeping. So when they don't know who is peeping their peeping, only that it's been peeped, they have to stop peeping."

"Right!" Kwami almost gave Judy five but then gave it to himself instead and Judy gave herself five.

"Could one of you Martians break that down into plain Ronald MacDonald English?" Kitty asked.

"If they know that somebody's on to them they'll probably stop," Judy said. "They probably figure it's the FBI or somebody."

"So what we do is to send them a letter or something saying that we're wise to their little tricks and they better check themselves out."

"Right." Kwami had a big smile on his face. "And we can sign the letter something like 'a well-meaning friend.' I dug that in a flick once when this chick sent a letter to another chick saying that her husband was fooling around with somebody and then she signed it 'a well-meaning friend.' "

"I don't think we should send a letter," Anthony said. "I saw in one of the FBI pictures once where some guy sent a letter demanding some ransom and they traced the letter. In no time at all they knew where the guy had bought the paper, what kind of typewriter he used, that he was right handed."

"That's right, a letter could be dangerous," I said. "I heard of a case once when a guy demanded ransom and sent a note and they figured out he was left handed, tall, and liked chicken noodle soup."

"How did they know he liked chicken noodle soup?" Kitty asked.

"Because that's what he wanted the ransom paid off in!" I said, laughing.

We decided to make some phone calls. Judy was elected to make the first call. She put a handkerchief over the mouthpiece of the telephone and spoke in a slight accent.

"Allo?" Judy made a funny face as she spoke. "We vant to let you know that ve are vise to you. Vat? Is this 555-2167? Oh, sorry."

She finally got the right number and called four times, each time using a different voice. Each call was exactly one minute long at the most so it couldn't be traced, and each one was made from a different phone booth.

Two days later the Russians showed up again.

"There's got to be either one of two explanations," Leslie concluded. "Either the secret is so important that they're going to take a chance, or they're dumb."

"Maybe we should just walk up to them and tell them that we know all about their secret plans?"

"What secret plans?" I asked.

"If they're Russians they got to have some secret plans," Kwami continued. "The first thing you got to have if you're a Russian is a secret plan."

"I ain't walking up to no Russians and saying nothing!" Anthony said.

"I'll do it," Wayne said.

"You're gonna walk right up to the Russians and tell them that you have their secret plans?" Kitty asked. You could tell Kitty didn't believe that Wayne had the nerve.

"Yeah,'" Wayne answered. He started tying his shoes even though they were already tied and you could tell he was having second thoughts about the whole thing. "Why not?"

"You know, Wayne," I said. "Russians are badder than waterbugs."

Kitty cracked up when I said that. So did Anthony, but I was more interested in Kitty thinking it was funny. But Wayne had that funny look on his face and I knew that he was going to do it.

When the Russians came again it was Leslie that saw them first, sitting outside of Willie's place waiting for him to show up. Wayne was in Frankie's eating a slice of pepperoni pizza when Leslie came to get him. He finished the pizza and gulped a mouthful of soda to wash it down as Leslie dragged him out of the door. One of the Russians was out of the car, leaning against the front fender.

"Hi." Wayne raised his hand as if the Russians were far away.

"Hello." The Russian smiled with the bottom half of his face. His eyes stared straight at Wayne, giving him cold chills.

"You have the same kind of car that those other guys have," Wayne said. "You know, the FBI or what do you call those guys?"

"The FBI?" the Russian answered. His eyes never left Wayne.

"Yeah."

"What is your name?" the Russian asked. "I am Constantine Oblenenov."

"My name is Douglass, right, that's what it is, Frederick Douglass."

"What do you do, Frederick?" Constantine asked. "Do you play sports?"

"Well, sometimes."

"Do you live around here?"

"Yeah."

"How old are you?"

"Twelve."

"What do you study in school?"

"Oh, math and science."

"What do you study in science?"

"Mostly about rockets and that kind of stuff this year. Next year we're going to be studying electronics."

"Oh, that's quite good."

"Hey, Wayne, your mother's calling you," Kwami called to Wayne.

"My mother? I don't hear my mother calling me," he answered.

"I know, she's around the corner."

"No, she's not, she's at work."

"I just saw her around the corner."

"I'll see you later," Wayne said to Constantine, and walked back to where we were waiting.

"How can you hear my mother all the way around the—"

"Shut up. You realize what just happened?"

"What?"

"You were just telling that Russian everything you know."

"I wasn't telling him anything except that the FBI had a car like his. I figured that if I mentioned the FBI he'd get scared."

"Oh, yeah. That's all you told him?"

"Yeah."

"You didn't tell him what you were studying in school?"

"He just asked if . . . . oh, oh."

"And you told him you were studying about rockets and his eyes lit up, right?" I said.

"Oh, man. You even told him what you were going to be studying next year," Kwami said. "Now they got the whole American educational system down to a T."

"No wonder Willie talks so much," Wayne said. "I thought the guy was just being friendly."

"Yeah, well, you sure blew that. It's fairly plain that we can't trust anyone to talk to them face to face," Leslie said.

"Not me, anyway," Wayne said and sighed.

The Russians didn't show up for two days, and we began to think that perhaps Wayne's talk did more good than we thought. That was the same weekend, however, that we saw the Russian that had been leaning against the car talking to Wayne on television. What's more, he was at a party given for some bigwigs in Washington, D.C., and the President was there as well. Judy, Kitty, Anthony, and me had seen Constantine on television. Kwami's team had a game that evening so he missed it and everybody else that had been watching television had been watching *Earthquake,* a movie. Kwami said that one good thing about it was that they had changed their base of operations from New York to Washington. Anthony said that was even worse because they were down there messing with the President. It didn't make that much difference either way though, because the next day the Russians were back in front of Willie's house.

We tried to decide what to do next. Kwami was for sending some more messages to the Russians, but Judy and Kitty were against it.

"They probably don't understand what you're talking about," Judy said.

"They speak perfect English."

"Yeah, they talk English but they probably think in Russian. That's why they don't understand what we're trying to tell them."

"That's nonsense," Kwami said. "If they can make a monkey understand people and even do some little jive talking, you can make a Russian understand."

"Monkeys don't really understand the same way that people do, though," Judy said. "If they did, they'd be people."

"I know a guy I'm not too sure about," Wayne threw in.

"You can make a monkey understand what you're talking about and you can make a horse or a dog or just about anything understand you if you put your mind to it," Kwami said. "And I know that the Russians are smarter than dogs and monkeys. They're just being smart, and making believe that they don't understand to find out how much we really know."

"I don't think so," Judy said. "I know it's not doing us any good but what we have is a communications problem, I think. You can't make people understand you all the time. And I don't really think that you can make animals understand either. I love my dog, Major, but he really doesn't understand anything I say."

"I think he does." I said.

"I doubt it." Judy was shaking her head. "I doubt it."

Seven

In one day I had a bad thing happen to me and a funny thing happen. Now, that's not so unusual in itself, only the two were connected to a third thing which was the biggest thing that ever happened to me. Let me tell you about the third thing first and then go back and tell you about the first two.

The third thing was that I found out that I didn't know Kwami Green. That's right, I didn't know him at all. Oh, I knew what he looked like and everything, but I didn't know what was inside of him until the day that his father got mad at him for not cleaning up his room.

"So I said, 'Pop, I'm going to clean the room up.' And then he says that I shouldn't clean it up. Please don't clean it up, and things like that. So I get up to go clean the room up, see?" Kwami's eyes were reddish and I knew that he was really upset. I thought he might even cry. "So he pushes me back down on the chair and starts saying things like it ain't right for a guy as young and healthy as I am to have to strain myself picking up socks and everything when my mother could do it.

"I had just come in from Milbank, right? And he was standing in the living room so I didn't have a chance to know what was going on or anything, and there was no one downstairs on the stoop. So he's going through all this garbage and then I get mad and catch an attitude. So he says to me 'would you like a glass of soda?' So I come back and say 'yeah.' You know, because I was mad. I figured he didn't have to go through all that non-sense, you know.

"So he goes on into the kitchen and brings me a glass of water. And I'm sitting there like a fool drinking this water and he's standing there looking at me. So then . . . " Kwami shut up for a while.

"How come you wanted me to bring Major over?" Judy asked, trying to fill up the quiet spot in the conversation.

"Anyway." Kwami started talking again. "Then he

says something about being sorry that my mother wasn't home so she could bring the water to me. He said he was sorry that she was still in the hospital for tests. I looked at him. I didn't know what he was talking about. Then he tells me that my mom had to go to the hospital with chest pains. Wow, man. She was in my room cleaning up and whatnot and all of a sudden she got some pains in her chest and he took her to the hospital."

No one said anything for a while because everyone was afraid to ask how his mother was. Finally Judy asked him was she okay and Kwami nodded that she was.

"She came home later on and said that the doctor told her to take it easy for a while. She's got high blood pressure and he gave her some medicine to keep that down and a diet. But you know, my father tried to make it seem like it was my fault or something. All night long he was saying things like 'anything you want your mother to do for you, sir,' and that kind of jive. I really feel like moving out."

"What picture was he talking about?" Kitty asked. "When you and him came out of the house he was talking about some picture. Wasn't he?"

"Yeah, I took the picture down and threw it away."

"You mean that picture that you had on your wall over the bowling trophy?" Wayne asked.

Kwami nodded that that was the picture.

"That was just a picture of a movie star." Wayne's voice was so high he sounded like a girl.

"Yeah, but she was white," Kwami said. "I had a picture of Freda Payne, one of Natalie Cole, and one of the Bionic Woman. Petey Johnson borrowed the pictures of the two sisters 'cause he wanted to re-photograph them and put them in one of those collages he's always making. So he comes in and jumps all over that."

" 'Cause you had a picture of a white girl on your wall?" Judy asked.

"Didn't I just say that?" Kwami gave Judy a look.

"That ain't nothing," Kitty said. "Judy's father had a fit because she had a picture of Kwami on her wall that she got from the school newspaper."

"That's right. He said he didn't want no kinky-haired grandchildren."

"He said *what?*" Kwami looked at Judy.

"He's as bad as your father, huh?" Kitty stuck in the right words just in time. Kwami shook his head.

"Let's get on with the project at hand," Kwami said. "This is getting a bit too heavy."

The project at hand was teaching Major to talk. It was mainly my idea, but Kwami tried to take credit for it. After the problems we had had in trying to get the Russians to understand that we knew what they were up to, we had got into this big argument about communicating with other people. Kwami said that you could communicate with anything if you knew how to. He had read this article in an old issue of *New York* magazine where some people were teaching a monkey to talk. Now Kwami figured that a dog must be smarter than a monkey. I told him that I had learned in biology that monkeys were the next smartest things to people. He said that if monkeys were so smart how come they didn't live in apartments like dogs did. He said he saw a program about dogs once and that some dogs got a lot of money left to them when their owners died.

"Some of those dogs are millionaires," Kwami said. "I ain't no millionaire and I ain't never read about no monkey millionaire, either. Which is why I say that dogs is smarter than monkeys."

It didn't make a lot of book sense but it made a lot of seeing-is-believing sense. So when I thought about trying to teach Major to talk, I knew Kwami would go for the idea. As I said, he even tried to take credit for it.

We decided to take Major up to Leslie's house to teach him how to talk. The reason we decided to take him to Leslie's house was Leslie's grandmother stayed with them, and anytime you went to her house her grandmother would always come up with sandwiches or something.

Leslie had to go up first and make sure it was okay, and Kwami had to go home and tell his mother where he would be, and Judy took Major for a short walk while she was waiting for everyone to get ready. Anthony and Wayne were playing handball and that left me and Kitty on the stoop. Me and Kitty and the beginning of the worst day in my life. Or, if not the worst day, at least the most embarrassing moment.

Kitty had this book of word games she was doing.

What you had to do was unscramble a word. Like
LOTEH is HOTEL scrambled. So she was doing these
and I was thinking about how she had held my hand
that time in the park and how I really liked her. I was
thinking about Judy having a picture of Kwami, too,
and it all seemed pretty nice. So I asked Kitty if she
wanted a picture of me.

"A picture of you?" She turned toward me real slow.

"Yeah." I was still feeling pretty good.

"What would I want a picture of you for?" she asked.

"Well, you could put it up on your wall or something,"
I said.

"Oh, I see," Kitty said. She was smiling a little and
so I smiled a little, too. "And we could kind of be boy-
friend and girl friend."

"Yeah, kind of."

I was just about ready to figure out what picture I
was going to give her when Kitty started laughing. She
dropped her book and her pencil and really started to
crack up. Then she rolled off the stoop and lay on the
sidewalk. I never saw anybody laugh so hard. Wayne
and Anthony came over and asked me what happened,
and I said I didn't know. They tried to ask Kitty but
she kept on laughing until the tears ran down her face.
Finally she stopped enough to get back on the stoop and
then she looked over at me and started laughing again
until she was really crying.

Judy got back the same time that Leslie did. They
asked Kitty what she was laughing about.

"This character wants me to . . . " She slapped her leg and started laughing again.

By this time I was really feeling bad because everyone was asking me why Kitty was laughing and naturally I didn't want to tell them.

"This character . . . " Kitty started telling what had happened again and was pointing at me.

"This character wants me to be his girl friend and hang his picture on my wall." Kitty finished just in time for more laughter to come out.

Wayne started laughing, and Anthony started laughing, and Leslie just kind of held her hand over her mouth and started giggling. I also knew that when Kwami got back I'd have to go through the whole thing all over again.

I was right. After they told him why Kitty was laughing, Kwami said, "When you people getting married, man?" Kwami and his big mouth.

Kwami put his hand on my shoulder and I pushed it off.

"Oh, I see, only Kitty can put her hand on your shoulder," he said. "I can understand that."

Then everybody started to crack up again. Now that's what I mean when I said I found out that I didn't understand Kwami. First he was all sad and everything about his mother and really seemed like he was okay. Then the first chance he got he started cracking up on me because of that stupid thing I said to Kitty. We started up the stairs to Leslie's house and they were still on my case. I would have liked to punch out Kwami and Kitty right then and there. I really didn't think I was good enough to beat Kwami though—in fact, I was pretty sure that I wasn't. I had had a fight with Kitty about a year ago and it came out even, but she had gotten taller so I just tried to forget about the whole thing. At least when we started teaching Major to talk they got off me.

"The first thing we got to do," said Kwami, "is to decide what he's going to say."

"Seems to me that if he says anything he'll be just about the coolest dog in the world," Kitty said.

" 'Cause he's not a puppy, see?" Kwami lifted Major's chin slightly and looked at the dog as he spoke. "If he was a puppy you could teach him to say anything because he couldn't know any better. But he knows a lot of things, now, so you got to be careful. Say you try to teach him to ask for a piece of fried chicken and he don't like fried chicken. He might not say anything just because he don't like what you're trying to teach him to say, dig?"

"Suppose he don't speak English?" Wayne asked.

"Don't be dumb, Wayne. American dogs all understand American and that's what we're going to teach Major to speak." Kwami gave Wayne a mean look. "And if you come up with one more dumb statement I'm going to wait till the next time it rains and then turn your nose upside down and drown you."

"So what are we going to teach Major to say?" I asked.

"Something patriotic," Kwami said. "So he'll feel good saying it."

"How about 'Give me liberty or give me death'?"

"He might think we're trying to bump him off."

"How about, 'I regret that I have only one life—' "

"There you go with that dying stuff again," said Kwami.

"All that good patriotic stuff is about being dead or how you gonna die if something don't happen." Wayne was beginning to whine. Wayne always whined when somebody got on him.

"How about 'tip-a-canoe and Tyler too'?"

"What's that mean?"

"I don't know. But it's got to be famous 'cause we learned it in history."

"The only thing you got to be to be famous in history is dead a bunch of years."

"I have it. How about 'Don't tread on me'?"

That was the famous American saying that we decided we would teach Major. The first thing that we did was to write the words on four large pieces of paper. Then Kwami and Kitty took turns reading the words to Major as Judy held him in her arms.

"Don't," Kwami said. He looked at Major and the dog seemed to understand him.

"Tread." Major still looked at Kwami.

"On." Major's tail began to wag.

"Me." Major squirmed.

"Now comes the hard part," Kitty said.

"You meaning getting my main dog here to talk?"

"No, just getting him to try," Kitty answered. "Dogs have been treated so badly over the years that they don't even try to talk. People usually just tell them to do things like sit down, and heel, and play dead, or get off the sidewalk that that's what they think they're supposed to be doing. We got to convince Major that he's really supposed to talk."

"Leave that to the big K," Kwami said. "Kwami Green, teacher of frogs and dogs. Kwami Green, teacher supreme. Not only will I have your frog hopping, I'll get his foot to pattin' and not only will your dog talk, he'll speak Pig Latin."

"Don't be telling us that jive, tell Major," Judy said.

Kwami knelt down in front of Major and looked him right in the eye.

"Not only can you talk if you want to, Major, but you can converse on any level on which you choose. Now, dig, watch Kwami's lips as he speaks and then you repeat after me. Don't feel self-conscious if you don't get it right the first time 'cause I got until nearly three o'clock to get you together. Now, repeat after me: Don't . . . . tread . . . . on . . . . me."

Major just looked at Kwami and wagged his tail.

Kwami got a little closer to Major until their noses were almost touching. "Look into my eyes and believe you can talk, dog," Kwami said. "I'm not teaching you anything jive to say. I'm teaching you some good stuff. This is a famous American saying. Now, I'm going to lift my head a little so you can watch my lips. See." Kwami lifted his head so that Major could see his lips. "Now repeat after me." Kwami moved his lips in slow, exaggerated movements as he repeated the phrase. "Don't . . . tread . . . on . . . me!"

Major barked once.

"I think he got it!" Kwami said.

"All he said was woof!"

"He's warming up," Kwami said. "Give him a little time. What's the first thing that you said when you started talking, turkey. You probably couldn't even say woof."

"Don't . . . tread . . . on . . . me!"

Major got closer to Kwami and licked him on the mouth. Kwami didn't move.

"Oh, sweat!" Wayne said. "Major kissed Kwami right on the lips and Kwami didn't even move."

"I can't reject him at this crucial point, man," Kwami said, but he looked a bit uncomfortable. "That would be like leaving a kid back in kindergarten.

"Don't . . . tread . . . on . . . me!"

Major licked Kwami's face again.

"I think Major's in love with Kwami." Judy grinned.

"And by the way Kwami is taking his kisses, I think we may have something going."

"That's what's wrong with you people." Kwami jumped up. "Anytime you try to do something serious you people start clowning around. You don't know nothing about no psychology or nothing. I give up."

Kwami sat down on a hassock and ate one of the grilled cheese sandwiches Leslie's grandmother had made. It was obvious that he was mad.

"Don't get upset, Kwami," Kitty said. "Maybe it just takes a while. We'll try again some other time."

"He might be ready to talk now," Judy said, "and just waiting for the right time. I know a woman who had a little boy who didn't talk until he was almost seven years old and then he just started talking one day like he had been talking all along."

"That's right," Leslie added. "I've heard of that kind of thing happening myself. He may get up in the middle of the night and start talking."

"You know, I was thinking," I said. "Maybe you made more progress than you think you did."

"What do you mean?" asked Kwami.

"Well, what's the saying you were trying to teach him?"

"Don't tread on me," answered Kwami.

"Well, he didn't tread on you, did he?"

Kwami just sighed.

That night I got home and my father was all set to

have one of his "meaningful" conversations with me. We had one about twice a month. He usually gets on this real calm attitude and asks me something like what I thought of the crises in South Africa, or the abortion issue, or some other good doing thing like that. Only halfway through my answer, he would interrupt to tell me what he thought and that would be the end of the conversation. I'd sit there and listen until he was satisfied, then it would be over. Sometimes, just to be different, he would start the conversation off by asking me what I did that day. Then he would tell me what I should have been doing to better myself and what he would have been doing if he had been me. Then he'd watch television until he fell asleep in his chair.

This was one of those days when he was asking about what I did during the day so I told him about trying to teach Major to talk.

"Trying to do what?" he asked.

"Trying to teach Major to talk," I repeated.

"Okay." He nodded his head up and down, but I knew he didn't believe a word I was saying. "Major is that little blond girl's dog, isn't he?"

"Yep," I said, really enjoying the fact that he didn't know what was going on.

"Well, okay," he said, switching on the television. "I guess you know what you're doing. By the way, there's something on your dresser for you. It was pushed under the door."

On the dresser was a white envelope with my name

on it. Inside the envelope was a picture of Kitty. On the back it said 'to my friend, Dean.' Things were looking up.

"Mama Doc? Where are you? What are you doing under there? Are you sick? You sure don't look good. I'll have to make you some dill tea. Open your mouth."

Drusilla picked Mama Doc up and tried to peer into her mouth, but the big cat just meowed plaintively and hung limply in her arms.

"Um-hm, somebody trying to put something on this house and it's affecting you. That's what the matter is."

Drusilla went to the closet and got a handful of flour and went to the door. She sprinkled some just inside the door and then opened it and sprinkled some outside. Then she closed and bolted the door and put on two pots of water. She took a black candle and lit it and put it in the middle of the table. "If anybody or anything's in here I'll find out about it," Drusilla said, sitting at one end of the table. "Both of us will know it. Though I don't know who would be messin' with me. I ain't brought no harm to nobody. That old Lucas woman was looking funny at me the other day. I swear she's a West Indian. You got to be careful of them people, Mama Doc. They got more roots burning than you can shake a stick at."

Drusilla poured some dill into the water just as

bubbles began to appear in it.

"This dill will make you feel a lot better, Mama Doc. Did I tell you them white people that Willie wanted me to talk to weren't even from this country? Well, they weren't. I don't really like them 'cause they smile too much. You can't trust people who smile too much. Anyway, they were telling Willie that they thought that I was some kind of a scientist. But all they really want to do is to pump me and Willie for information."

Drusilla took some dried grass and put it into the pot not containing the dill and quickly turned off the heat. She stared into the pot as the grass turned slowly in the hot water. A full minute passed before she emptied the entire pot into the sink.

"Nothing much to worry about, Mama Doc," she said. "Just somebody being stupid, that's all. Now you come have some of this tea and you'll feel a lot better."

Eight

It was really the first good idea that Wayne had had in about three years. The last good idea he had was for the class to go to a movie for their class outing in the third grade (which was what the teacher wanted to do) instead of having a picnic (which was what the class wanted to do). It seemed like a terrible idea when the teacher first suggested it, and everyone in the class was sure that she would change her mind when she found out that they were all against it. But then Wayne said that it was a good idea and she said that they would go to a movie instead. Needless to say, everybody was pretty mad at Wayne.

After school they asked him why he hadn't stuck with the rest of the class and he said he thought it was going to rain. Now that seemed like a pretty dumb idea, too, because the class-day outing was three weeks away. At least it seemed dumb until the morning that they were supposed to go. It started raining at six o'clock that morning and by the time they got into the theater it was pouring. If they had scheduled the picnic they would have had to cancel the class outing altogether. Anyway, the movie was pretty good, too.

This idea of Wayne's came from a television advertisement he had seen. Some company was selling records and tapes that people were supposed to play when they went to sleep, and the records would teach them things which would stay in their minds when they woke up. What they were telling people was not to eat too much, or something like that, Wayne said, because it was designed for fat people. It would make them feel guilty whenever they ate. Wayne said that the man on television called it subliminal suggestion.

"What are you talking about, Wayne?" Kwami asked.

"Well, if we can't get the Russians to understand that we're on to them maybe we can subliminal Willie." Wayne was excited about his new idea.

"You mean wait until he falls asleep and run it down to him?" Kwami asked.

"Yeah," Wayne answered. "And then when he woke up he wouldn't even know why he knows what he knows."

"What're you going to do, Wayne," Judy asked, "go downstairs and knock on his door and say, 'Hey, Willie, go to sleep, man, I got something to tell you'?"

"If we could get one of them tape recorders we could do it like that," Wayne said. "Then we could hide it under his bed."

"Who's gonna be under the bed to turn it on?" Kitty looked at Wayne. " 'Cause you got to wait until the dude goes to sleep before you turn it on, right?"

"Maybe we could get him to give us a call just before he goes to sleep, see"—Anthony was beginning to enjoy putting Wayne on—"and then when he says he's just about ready to go to sleep we'll say would you mind just reaching under the bed and switching on the tape recorder, please."

"Yeah," Kitty added. "We want to make a recording of you snoring."

Everybody started laughing and slapping hands and everything and generally goofing when suddenly Kwami got the rest of the idea. He had his hand in the air, just ready to lay five on me, when the idea hit him. He got that funny look on his face which he always did when he was thinking. It looked as if he might be in a little pain.

"Intercoms!" Kwami suddenly shouted.

Kitty dropped her soda.

"What?"

"Intercoms!" Kwami said again. "We could plant some intercoms in Willie's bedroom, see, and late at night we could call down and give him the message while he's sleeping."

"You mean put them under his bed?" I asked.

"One under his bed and maybe one in his closet!"

"You know Sam Jones?" Kitty asked suddenly.

"Yeah," Kwami said, somewhat annoyed because he still wanted to talk about his idea.

"Well, he had this intercom thing that he hooked up in school for a play when the seniors had their presentation about two years ago. Then one time he hooked it up at a party. You talk into a microphone and it comes out over this speaker. He told my sister that you could hook up about four speakers to it," Kitty said. "I saw him hook it up once. I think I could do it if we can get his father to lend it to us."

"He's still away at school, right?" Anthony asked.

"Yeah," Kwami said, "but his father likes me. We can borrow it and then sneak it into Willie's place. If we can hook up four speakers around the room, it'll be boss."

"And then we can just wait until he goes to sleep and start rapping to him," Anthony said.

"How we gonna run all them wires in his house and who's gonna do the talking?" Wayne asked. "I ain't going down there again."

"We don't have to hook any wires into his bedroom.

All we have to do is to put one of the intercoms into his basement near the door and hook the wires from there into Leslie's house. We can run them along the drain pipe so he won't notice them. Then we can put speakers in his bedroom and they'll pick up anything we say as long as it's not more than fifty feet away. I can do some wiring. All we got to do is to get into Willie's place and hook it up."

"Yeah, that's all we got to do."

"I don't see how come you people are so scared," Judy said. "I wouldn't be scared."

"Okay, Miss Blue Eyes—you and me will do the hooking up tomorrow morning when Long Willie goes to work," Kwami said.

"If you can get the stuff from Sam's father," Kitty added.

"Right."

"That's cool with me," Judy said. "Things just don't scare me like that."

"We'll see, Judy," Kwami said. "We'll see."

It turned out Sam Jones' father did lend Kwami the intercom set and the next morning after Willie had left for work, we all set out to place the speakers in Willie's bedroom.

Anthony was the front door lookout and Kitty was the back door lookout. We had three walkie-talkies— Kitty had one, Anthony had one, and Judy carried the other one with her. We weren't taking any chances.

Leslie said she had seen Drusilla waiting at the bus

stop in front of her house that morning so she knew that no one was in Willie's place. Still, we all whispered as we took the shopping bag full of equipment into the basement.

Getting into the backyard was pretty easy. All we had to do was to go over to One Hundred Twenty-first Street near Light Billy's house and climb over two fences. Once we got over the two fences we looked up where Wayne was pointing from his window to Willie's door. Kwami reached up and sure enough, the key was there. Then he signaled Kitty and she dialed Willie's number. Kwami listened at the door to see if he heard the phone ringing in Willie's apartment. He did. He signaled that the phone was ringing and, figuring that Willie wasn't home because no one answered the phone, we started the second phase of the operation. Kwami signaled by lifting up three fingers, which meant that the number three man in the operation was to go into action. Instantly, Anthony went downstairs to the front and sat on the stoop. He had his two-way walkie-talkie with him. The other two-way walkie-talkie was being operated by Kitty in Leslie's apartment. If Anthony saw Willie coming he was going to tell Kitty who was going to signal us in Willie's apartment by throwing a marble against the door.

It was nearly five minutes before Anthony gave the all-clear signal from the stoop and Kitty hung up the phone. Kitty gave a clenched fist salute which was returned by Leslie down below, and Kwami put the key into the lock.

Kwami slipped in quietly and held the door open as Judy, Leslie, and me followed him in. There was an odd smell about Willie's place that Kwami had noticed once before on Willie's clothing. Leslie thought it might be some old dead animals that Drusilla used to fix people. When she said that, I felt a chill go down my back. We tipped quietly down a long hall which had one room on either side. At the end of the hall we could see the boiler room, its dim light barely making the peeling paint on the walls visible. Several roaches scurried out of our way as we crept toward the first room. When we got to it Kwami told me to push the door open.

"Why me?"

"Go on and push the door open, man." Kwami gave me a little push.

I took a deep breath and put my hand against the door. Slowly I pushed it open, listening to it creak. The room was dark and the smell, whatever it was, obviously came from somewhere inside of it.

I stepped in and swung my arms in front of me so I wouldn't bump into anything. I found a string that I figured must have been for the light and pulled it.

Leslie jumped as the light flooded the room and Kwami banged his funny bone into a pipe.

"What the heck is that thing?" Kwami pointed with his chin as he rubbed his elbow. I had never seen so much equipment in my life. There was a mass of tubes and pipes which curled around a small potbellied stove. The tubes were straight in some places and curled in others. Altogether the whole contraption stood about five feet high.

"They're probably making something that Willie saw in the laboratories on the job," Kwami said, inching closer to the tubing.

"What's in that thing over there?" There was a low grey tank from which the pipes and tubing seemed to come.

"That's where they put the chemicals and stuff."

"Open it up," I said.

"You open it up." Kwami stepped back.

"I'm not going to open it up. It could be acid or something."

"Or booby trapped."

"Smells like a still to me," Judy said.

"There's some more stuff over there." Kwami pointed to the other side of the room. There were piles of newspapers tied neatly against the wall and two large bags of charcoal. There was also a grey tub—it was uncovered. As we took a few steps toward it, Leslie first, then me, and then Kwami, in Indian file, we realized that it was the vat that was giving off the awful smells.

"Listen," Kwami raised his hand for silence. We were all silent. "You hear that ticking?"

It wasn't so much of a ticking as some very low clicking sounds that seemed to come from the vat.

"Oh, man, I think something's alive in there," Leslie said. "I think I'm going to faint."

"Let's get out of here," I said.

"No," Kwami protested, "we still got to check out the other room."

Against my better judgment, and especially against the fact that I had to go to the bathroom, we went out of the first room and down the hall to where Willie slept. The basement had about eight or nine different rooms, none of them connected. Willie said that some of the rooms used to be used to store coal before the building switched to oil heat. The walls along the hallway between the rooms were whitewashed and dirty. I could just imagine Drusilla walking from room to room in that grey robe of hers and being right at home.

In the other room which Willie used there was a red and black candle, about a foot high, burning on a small table. Behind the candle, eery in the flickering light, was a skull. Only it wasn't a human skull, I could tell. It might have been a dog's skull or some other animal's. I didn't know what kind of a skull it was and I wasn't particularly anxious to stick around and discuss the possibilities.

"Hey, man." Kwami took a step backward and pointed toward the skull. "What is that thing?"

Leslie walked over to where the skull was sitting and took a closer look at it.

"A skull," she said, turning to us.

Well, we knew that. None of us took our eyes off of it

either, at least not for very long. On the bed there was a quilt with a circle on it and four stars in exactly the same pattern that Leslie had drawn when we were trying to fix Major. There were more candles laying around and, in one corner, an old television set.

There was something that was covered by a sheet on one wall and we uncovered it carefully, pulling up one end of the sheet with a wire hanger that Kwami had straightened out. It just turned out to be Willie's clothes. Finding Willie's clothes under the sheet was kind of funny because we were almost too scared to lift the sheet at all. We relaxed for a bit before we saw Judy making frantic motions, pointing toward the door. We looked toward the door and there was nothing there, but then we saw Judy cupping her ears. We listened carefully and heard someone outside of the door leading into the backyard.

I tiptoed to the door and looked down the hallway. The light coming from beneath the door was interrupted by two shadows. Someone was standing in front of the door.

I motioned for the rest of them to follow me and I made my way back to the boiler room and we all crouched behind the huge water heater.

"Maybe it's Wayne," I whispered.

"Yeah, and maybe it's not," Leslie answered.

A moment later we heard more banging on the door and Drusilla's voice calling out to Willie.

"She can't get in," Kwami said, " 'cause I got the key."

"She can get in if she wants to badly enough," Leslie said. "Locks don't hold no Mojo people."

"Did you lock the door when you came in?" Judy asked.

"Uh-oh." Kwami looked at me and I looked back at him. We huddled a little closer.

Just then we heard the door open and the low shuffle of footsteps down the hall.

"Willie? Where you be? You in here?" Drusilla's voice was high and shaky. "You got somebody in here, Willie? Where you be, man?"

Her voice kept getting closer and closer as she came down the hall. We were as close as we could get behind the water heater and trying to get closer. The door to the boiler room opened and I could just picture Drusilla standing in the doorway, an evil look on her face and her hair going every which way. We held our breaths for a long minute and then the door closed. We could hear her footsteps going toward the front of the house and then her voice. I figured she must have been talking to Anthony.

We waited behind the boiler for what seemed forever before any of us dared to move or speak. If I had ever had any doubts about Mojo or anything else to do with magic, the skull in Willie's bedroom had changed my mind.

"I think she's gone," Kwami said, finally.

"What the heck happened to our lookouts?" Judy asked.

"I don't know." Kwami stood up and pulled his pants legs down and rubbed his knees. "Leslie, why don't you go out and check on Wayne and Anthony while the rest of us hook up the intercoms."

Leslie nodded that she would.

"And if we're not out of here in fifteen minutes call the FBI."

"The FBI?" Leslie looked at Kwami as if he were crazy.

Leslie went down the hall toward the back door and we watched her until she disappeared into the backyard. The thought occurred to me that Drusilla could have gotten Wayne and Anthony already and was just waiting outside to get Leslie and the rest of us as we came out. I didn't say anything to the others and tried to put it out of my mind.

"Men sure aren't neat," Judy said as we went back into Willie's bedroom.

"A lot of men are neat, dummy!" Kwami whispered back.

"Okay, okay, and don't be calling me no dummy," Judy said. "I'm as smart as you are and that's no lie."

"What we have to do is to put the speakers around the room and then put this amplifier somewhere nearby," Kwami explained. "Then when you talk, it comes into this amplifier and the speakers pick it up somehow. So the only thing we got to hook up is the amplifier."

"Does it have to be plugged in or anything?" I asked.

"Uh-uh. Only the one upstairs," Kwami said. "Look,

let's put one speaker behind the headboard and then we'll put one under the bed near the foot so he can't really tell where the sound is coming from."

Kwami went around to the front of the bed and carefully placed one of the small speakers behind Willie's headboard. It fit perfectly and couldn't be seen at all in the dim light. Then he went to the foot of the bed, carefully avoiding several chalk circles drawn in the middle of the floor, and started putting another speaker at the foot of the bed.

"How come you didn't step in them circles?" Judy asked.

"Just didn't, that's why," Kwami said. "You got that Scotch tape?"

"Here." Judy handed Kwami the tape. "What you mean you just didn't?"

"I just didn't that's all," Kwami said, fixing the speaker firmly in place at the foot of the bed.

"Well, why didn't you, that's what I want to know," Judy whispered.

"I don't know," Kwami whispered back, annoyed. "Look around for some more places to put the speakers. We can't stay in here all day, you know."

Judy looked around nervously. There was a closet near the corner of the room, next to the bureau which had a candle lit on it. Judy carefully walked over to the closet and climbed up on the bureau. She decided that it would be a good place to put a speaker. She forgot about the candle just long enough to knock it over.

She jumped down from the bureau and quickly put it upright. The candle was in a glass jar and Judy looked carefully to make sure that she hadn't broken the glass. She hadn't. What she had done, though, was to put the candle out.

Kwami had put another speaker over the electric meter, sticking it on with the tape. He came over to Judy as she stood in front of the candle. She looked whiter than she normally did.

"You think I should put one on top of the closet?" Kwami asked.

"I think so," Judy answered weakly.

Kwami jumped up on the bureau and put a speaker near the back of the closet. He covered it up with a newspaper.

"Kwami, the candle went out," Judy said.

"Light it with another candle. She got enough of them lit in here," Kwami said. "Place looks like a funeral home. I wouldn't go to sleep in here."

There was a pile of boxes in one corner of the room and Kwami thought of putting the amplifier there, but it was too far from the door. There was a covered night table near the door and Kwami looked under the cover. What it actually was was an orange crate that Willie had just covered to make himself a table. There were some magazines in the crate and an old pipe. Willie had probably forgotten they were even there. It was a perfect spot for the intercom speaker. Kwami put it in the crate, making sure that the switch was set in the On position.

Kwami and I hooked up the amplifier over the door leading out to the backyard. The amplifier was small and the hall was dark enough to hide it in the shadows if you weren't looking for it. He went outside and threw the wire up to Kitty. It took three throws before she got it. You could see it coming out of the basement so Kwami pushed it with a stick until most of it was hidden behind the drainpipe that came from the roof. Then Kitty pulled it in the window and took a beach towel and hung it out of the window, covering most of the wire. There were only a few feet of wire showing now.

We went back into Willie's place to make sure that the speakers were hidden and saw Judy standing just where we had left her.

"We got the wires up to Leslie's house," Kwami said. "Kitty just pulled them in the window. You can't see a thing, hardly."

"I don't think I should have stepped in those circles," Judy said.

"Yeah, well, come on out here and see if you can see the wire," Kwami said.

Judy didn't move.

"Come on, girl." Kwami beckoned her. "We don't have all day, you know."

"And I put the candle out!" Judy was still whispering, and we could see something was very much wrong.

"Okay, okay," Kwami said. "But let's check the wires out so we can split."

"I can't," Judy said.

"You what?"

"I can't move." There were tears running down Judy's face. "I'm fixed."

"You're what?" I looked at her. She was crying, but except for a little movement in her shoulders when she sniffled, she was frozen to the spot.

"I can't move," Judy wailed. "I can't even turn my head. I'm fixed."

"Then I guess we'll just have to leave you here until Drusilla drops by," Kwami said. "She'll be able to get you moving, I'm sure. I can see the headlines now. White girl gets fixed in ghetto! Police arrest Mojo candle!"

"Please Kwami, do something."

Kwami tried to pull Judy's foot forward but it didn't work. Even though he could move it a little she couldn't move it by herself at all.

"Try, Judy!" Kwami said.

"I'm trying," Judy said, through her tears.

Kwami got down on the floor and started walking Judy, putting first one foot in front and then the other as he got her started slowly toward the door. Each move seemed to take forever.

"Did I ever tell you that you got some skinny legs, Judy?" Kwami asked. "Your legs are almost as skinny as mine. Except mine are better looking because naturally I'm better looking than you are."

Just then there was a crackling noise in Judy's back pocket.

"Oh, oh, now you're really in trouble," Kwami said. "She's got you talking out of the wrong end."

"The walkie-talkie!" It had been Anthony's idea to bring them.

"Oh." Kwami stood up with a big smile on his face. "For a while there I thought you were in a worse fix than you thought you were in." Kwami took the walkie-talkie from Judy's pocket, switched it to the Speak position, and spoke into the transmitter.

"Operation Brother Bad. Lieutenant Kwami here," he said. "What's up?"

"Anthony just spotted Willie and Drusilla coming across Morningside Avenue." The voice crackled urgently from the walkie-talkie set.

Kwami swallowed hard and looked at Judy, then at me, and then back at Judy. Then he dropped to his knees and started walking her, one foot at a time, toward the door. We could still hear Leslie's voice over the walkie-talkie which Kwami had stuffed back into Judy's pocket.

"They're coming down the street!"

Kwami walked Judy a few more furious steps and then stood up, put his arm around her waist, and carried her stiffly from Willie's basement apartment. I locked the door and put the key back where we had found it, and the two of us started carrying Judy, stiff as a board, toward the basement of Three Fifty-six where we could pass through to the street. By the time we got out into the street again, the sweat was pouring off Kwami. We made it to the front of the block just in time to see Willie and Drusilla disappear through Willie's front door.

We still had to get Judy up to Leslie's house. Mrs Griffith, Wayne's mother, was just coming home from shopping, and she stopped to look at us carrying Judy.

"Hello, Mrs. Griffith." Kwami stopped, lowered his head, and wiggled his shoulders twice. "We're practicing this new dance. It's called the Funky Zombie."

Mrs. Griffith gave him that sideways look grown-ups always get when they think they're being made fun of but aren't too sure.

Anthony met us at the stoop. "Hey, what happened?"

"Don't ask no questions now," Kwami said. "Just help me to get this crazy chick into the house."

It took four cups of hot tea with lemon, a twelve-ounce Pepsi-Cola, and all of Leslie's power (which consisted mainly of rubbing chicken fat on the back of the neck and a lot of humming) to bring Judy back to the point where she could walk again. Anthony said that he thought she was just scared, not really fixed, and Wayne thought that the two might not be too far apart.

"If Kwami hadn't gotten me out of there I'd probably be dead right now," Judy said.

"Did you get everything planted?" Kitty asked.

"Yeah," Kwami said. "No thanks to old blue eyes here. I told her to keep out of the circles. Oh, no, she had to walk around in the circles and then she put the candle out."

"Kwami, whatever-your-middle-name-is Green, you're a bald-faced liar." Judy put down her cup and squinted her eyes. "You didn't no more tell me to not walk in those darn circles than take wings and fly. And you know that's the truth, too."

"Well, if you had any sense you wouldn't of walked into them," Kwami said. That was about two seconds before the cops arrived.

Nine

⫷ I was the first to hear the sirens and looked out the front window. There were already three patrol cars in front blocking the street and policemen everywhere. Some people were pointing toward Leslie's front window. I had just pulled the curtain shut when the knock came on the door.

"It's the cops," I said.

"What do they want?" Kwami asked.

"Oh, sweat, Willie probably called the police," Wayne

said. "I think I better go home."

"Shut up, Wayne," Judy said. "If Willie called the police, and you leave, we'll say you did it."

"Yeah," Anthony joined in, "we'll blame the whole thing on you."

The knock came on the door again, and a heavy voice announced that it was the police.

Kwami made quick motions for everybody to gather in the center of the room.

"We all say we don't know anything about anybody breaking into Willie's place, right?"

Everyone nodded.

"And the first person that says anything, the rest of us blame it on them. Okay?"

Again we nodded.

"Good, now look natural as Leslie opens the door."

Everyone sat around and tried to look as natural as possible as Leslie, walking as naturally as she could, opened the door in a very natural manner, and asked the policemen what it was they wanted as naturally as she could.

"We got a report that a young girl was forcibly carried into one of these buildings." The heavy, red-faced policeman looked over Leslie's shoulder at the rest of the group. "Mind if I come in?" he asked.

Leslie stepped away from the door and three police officers, two white and one black, came in.

One of the officers walked right over to Judy.

"Are you all right, miss?" he asked.

"Me?" Judy swallowed hard. "I didn't do anything."

"That's right," Kwami said, "we're all innocent until proven guilty. And I can vouch for her. She didn't do nothing 'cause she was sitting here the whole time it happened."

"We got a report that a young Caucasian girl was carried into this building by three black males," the officer continued. "Are you sure you're okay?"

"You got a report what?" Kwami stood up.

"Shut up, kid," the other white policeman said.

"Hey, brother"—Kwami turned to the black officer—"are you going to let them talk to me like that?"

"You know that girl?" the black officer asked.

"Wait a minute," Kitty said. "You mean you heard about a white girl being carried in here by three black dudes?"

"That's right," the officer said.

"Well, that's me," Kitty said. "They just carried me in about ten or fifteen minutes ago because I was tired. I'm the white girl you're looking for, but don't worry about nothing because I'm okay, officers."

"You okay, miss?" The white officer turned back to Judy, ignoring Kitty.

"Who, me?" Judy asked.

"You're the only . . . " He looked at Kitty. "You do fit the description."

"Except I'm not white," Judy said. "She's the only white girl here."

"What school do you go to?" the cop asked.

"I.S. 201," Judy answered.

"And you?" he asked Kitty.

"I.S. 201."

"What's up?" Another police officer came in. This one had stripes on his arm. The first officer whispered something to him, and the four of them whispered together. Then they took everybody's name and address, and left. It had been fairly interesting for everybody except Wayne, who was scared. He looked out of Leslie's window and called after the policemen just before they drove away.

"Am I under arrest?" he called.

"Yes!" one of the white cops called out as they drove down the street. "Go to jail the first thing in the morning!"

"Mama Doc, you remember that little fool that nearly killed me with his bicycle? You remember, he come here with his little big-eyed self." Drusilla tried to get the hanger she was using for a television antenna just right as she talked to Mama Doc. "Well, he and his little fool friends been hanging around Willie's place. I don't know what they after. These children today would steal the pennies off a dead man's eyes. That's right. I come over to Willie's place and I hear this scurrying. At first I thought it was rats because these New York basements keep some rats. Anyway, I listen real close and I don't hear nothing else, so I go on and look around for Willie but he ain't there.

"Then I see this foot down behind the storage tank. I make believe I don't see it because it could be one of them thieves. So I pretended I didn't see nothing, and then I went out the front door and I could hear them scurrying out the back way. When I heard them I peeked back in, and it was some of those darn kid fools that Willie always be talking to. I told Willie and he said they just having their fun. Well, I told him that they could have all the fun they wanted with his stuff, but some of my stuff was down there, too. He couldn't hear nothing but started flapping his jaws about how the Russians were so excited about meeting me.

"Did I tell you I went up to their place? Or at least some house they have over near Central Park. They ask about Mojo again, and asked me if I believe it was real. Real? Mama Doc, are you real?"

Drusilla picked up Mama Doc and looked her in the eye. There was a low sound coming from deep within Mama Doc and her eyes were almost shut. Drusilla pulled the cat up against her and squeezed her gently. Then she put her on the floor.

"Now you just get on away from here, Mama Doc. I ain't gonna spoil you, and that's for sure. Anyway, everything I said they would be scribbling it down. Scribble, scribble, scribble. Some people believe if they write something down they know something about it. They don't know a bit more now than they ever did if you ask me. They say they got somebody else they want me to meet. I just bet they do, too.

"I wouldn't be doing none of this if it weren't for Willie. He says it's his one real chance to really do something for them kids. The way that man goes on about kids it's a wonder he ain't had a passel of them for himself. What was it before? Oh, yes, making that rotgut down in the basement and selling it to get money for trophies or something. Got the whole basement smelling like something died in it and was too ornery to get itself buried. Willie got a good heart though. I guess what the Lord took away from the man in brains, he made up for in heart.

"But I tell you, Mama Doc, if I catch them little fools messin' around with any of my stuff I'm gonna turn them every which way but loose, so help me."

Believe it or not, it was Kwami's father who came up with the idea for the voice that we were going to use on Willie. We were in Kwami's house—Kwami and his brother had to take turns staying home with their mother while their father worked—practicing different voices when Kwami's father came in and asked what we were doing.

"We're trying to get a spooky voice to try on somebody," Wayne blurted out.

"Why do you want to do that?" Mr. Green asked.

Wayne realized that he was talking too much and just shrugged his shoulders.

"Well." Mr. Green scratched at his chin. "If you want to get a real spooky voice why don't you use a tape recorder. You can do lots of things with a tape recorder."

We started thinking about it and started practicing to see how it would sound. At first it sounded the same as when we spoke naturally. But Leslie had one of the large tape recorders, which had two different speeds on it, and that's the one we finally used. We taped Leslie and Anthony speaking together with the tape on a high speed and then played it back at a low speed. It sounded just right.

That night we went over to Leslie's house, all except Kwami and Wayne, and waited until we figured Willie to be asleep. We had taped a two-minute message to Willie which we decided we'd play every ten minutes until our parents called us and made us come home, or until Leslie's grandmother put us out. We had told our parents that we were practicing for a play and that they could reach us at Leslie's house if they wanted to. We saw Willie go into the basement about ten o'clock and we waited until eleven before we sent the first message. We would have waited longer, but my mother and Kitty's mother had already called wondering when we were coming home. We didn't have to wait long to get the results of our message.

The message was down to the part about us knowing what Willie was doing and that he'd better mend his ways and make sure that no harm came to any of his friends (that was my idea), when we heard this screeching outside. We went to the window and looked out and saw all this commotion down in front of the house.

"Lord! What happened, child?" Mrs. Lambert was standing up with her hand to her head, and Mrs. Trevelyian and old man Turner were standing near her. They had knocked over one of the folding chairs they used to sit on in the evenings, and old man Turner had dropped his pipe. Willie was already across the street, wearing only his robe, looking back toward the basement apartment he had just come from. Old man Turner and the two elderly ladies rushed across the street, too. Anything that had scared Willie that bad they wanted to get away from.

"What's the matter with you, Willie?" Johnny Turner asked.

"There's voices in that apartment!" Willie said, gasping for breath. "They said they know all about me and that I'm gonna die."

"Child, death is chasing the man and here I am running with him!" Mrs. Lambert started running away from Willie.

"Ain't no death chasing me! Them's just voices!" Willie said.

"Oh, my God, death all over he face." Mrs. Lambert grabbed her massive bosom, turned her eyes toward heaven and fainted dead away.

Somebody called the police. Later, Wayne figured out

that there was someone on every block in the city whose only job was to call the police when anything happened.

When the police got there, they made Willie go back into his house and put some more clothes on, which wasn't very easy to do because Willie was pretty scared. The policemen that came in response to the call thought that Willie was just crazy and laughed among themselves. One of them told Willie that everything was all right, that he heard "voices" too. He told Willie that they came to him from out of a peanut butter jar and that Willie should check his house for peanut butter jars.

Most of the people in the neighborhood said that Willie was okay, that he wouldn't harm anybody, and the police didn't arrest him. They did go in with him while he got his clothes, and then told him to go sleep it off. Willie said he wasn't going back to that house anymore, at least not that night.

Half the block stayed awake for the rest of the night, trading theories about why Willie was running around half naked. Judy's mother and father came around just when all the cops were there, looking for Judy. They went to Kitty's house, but Mrs. Cumberbatch, Kitty's mother, said that she hadn't seen Judy at all that evening. Finally, Judy saw her mother's car out the window and went downstairs. She told her mother that some guy had gone crazy, and that she thought she should stay over at Kitty's house that night in case something else went on. There was a lot of talk, and finally Kitty went over to Judy's house to spend the night.

After everybody had left, and things had quieted down, Kwami and me went back into Willie's house and got Sam's intercom equipment out. We returned it the next day and got back to Leslie's house, which we were more or less using as headquarters, just as Judy and Kitty arrived. It was the busiest Saturday morning that we had had in a long while on that block with everyone oohing and aahhing about what had happened the night before. Mrs. Lambert, who had only spent about an hour in the hospital, said that she had seen death all over Willie's face. She said that Willie was going to die any day now and anybody with any sense had better stay away from him.

"Anyway," said Anthony, "it didn't work."

"What do you mean, it didn't work?" Leslie asked. "Willie heard us talking as plain as day."

"Yeah, but he thought it was some kind of ghost or something," Anthony said. "The whole idea was to get him to believe that he should stop passing around secrets. If he thinks it's a ghost or something, then it didn't work."

"Well, maybe he did get the message," Wayne suggested. "Let's see if those Russians come around anymore."

We got our answer the next day. At exactly twelve noon, the long, black limousine carrying the Russians pulled up in front of Willie's house. One of the Russians got out and went to Willie's door and rang the bell. There was no answer. He got back into the car and sat there about five minutes. The Operation Brother Bad group was sitting on the stoop across the street and we thought that maybe Willie had just decided not to show up anymore, when all of a sudden we saw Willie hustling around the corner. He was smiling at the Russians, and they got out of their car and started shaking hands with him as if nothing had changed. Willie went into his place with them, and they came out about fifteen minutes later carrying a big pile of yellow envelopes.

Kwami looked at me and I looked at Kwami. Nothing had changed. Willie was still dealing with the Russians. Fifteen minutes later, Drusilla showed up. She had a jar with her and a brown paper bag. She took some powder out of the bag and started sprinkling it around Willie's door. Then she started sprinkling something from the jar. It looked, at least from across the street where we were sitting, like blood.

"Human blood," said Wayne.

"How do you know it's human blood?" Judy asked.

"Do it look like chicken blood?" Wayne asked.

"Not particularly."

"See, I told you it was human blood."

They watched, and everybody else on the block watched. Drusilla was making big circles in front of Willie's place and sprinkling the liquid everywhere she went.

"She's probably putting a curse on the last person in the house on the night that Willie heard us on the intercom."

"That was those cops," said Wayne. "They went in and looked around after Willie left. They were the last ones in there."

"Except for me and Dean," Kwami said. "We went back in to get the intercom stuff."

"Who was the last one in?" Leslie asked.

"Well, I got the intercom and stuff and put everything in the shopping bag and so I guess I . . . oh, wait a minute, Dean, didn't you go back to get the one we left on the closet?"

I got a very sick feeling in the pit of my stomach, and for two cents I would have borrowed Kitty's bicycle and knocked Drusilla down again. I sat there trying to imagine what my skull would look like sitting up on Willie's dresser with a candle in front of it.

"Where you going, man?" Kwami asked as I stood up.

"Upstairs," I said. "I don't feel too good."

"You know, Mama Doc, you can believe just about half of what you hear in the light and just about nothing that you hear in the dark. Willie come busting over here the other night saying he heard these voices. He said somebody trying to put something on him. I don't know, Mama Doc. I never heard of any spirits announcing themselves in the middle of the night. If a spirit wants to get to you then it just *gets* to you. It don't stop to make some kind of speech the way Willie was talking about.

"Mama Doc, what are you thinking about? Just sitting up there on your shelf looking like you own half of New York City! That's one thing I like about you. Nothing bothers you. You're so highfalutin you probably think you're a queen or something.

"Willie run out his house in his robe—thank the Lord he stopped to put that on or he really would have those old biddies clucking—and half the block go running down the street with him. It sure must have been some kind of sight. They ain't got nothing better to do than to sit out there all night on the sidewalk anyway, hoping that something gonna happen for them to cluck about.

"Willie come over here looking all scared and acting like he about ten years old. 'Drusilla, they's voices in my room.' That's what he says.

" 'What they sound like?' I ask. He tell me they sound like they wanted to get him. Shoot. He was laying up there in his bed, with nothing on except his buck natural skin, 'sleep to the world, and they were *trying* to get him. A hard-of-hearing blind man on crutches could of got him if he wanted him. I wonder if them Russians is up to something. I heard they some sneaky devils. They got sneaky eyes, too. They try to act stupid like they don't know nothing but what day it is. You ask me, Mama Doc, they know the hour and the minute. Um-hm. Maybe even a little more than that, Mama Doc, maybe even a little more than that."

Ten

⌨ "There were Mojos," explained Leslie, "and then there were Mojos. When you invoked a Mojo, what you were really doing was making the undead do your bidding."

"The what?" Wayne asked. He had running in his eyes.

"The undead," Leslie repeated. "Those are the people who were evil when they were alive, and although they look like they are dead, are actually trapped between living and dying. Their souls have to wander around in the underworld forever, or at least until their evil is worked off."

"The underworld?" Kwami scratched his head.

"Not crooks," Leslie said. "The underworld is where your soul goes after you die if you've been evil."

"What's it like down there?" Wayne asked.

"How do I know?" Leslie replied. "The only thing I know is that if Drusilla is going to put a curse on Dean, we'd better get something going soon. Just the way that blood was dripping around, you know, when she was sprinkling it and everything."

"Yeah."

"Well, if we don't get this whole thing resolved pretty soon that's just the way Dean's blood is going to be dripping around."

"Wow. Thanks a lot, Leslie. I really needed to know about that," I said. "I mean, I really wanted to know how my blood is going to be dripping around."

"It's not my fault that you got yourself doomed, turkey!" Leslie looked hurt. "I didn't tell you to start a war with a Mojo woman."

"Hey, let's not go through this again," Kwami said. "We have to get things together now before they get out of hand. We got to turn everything over to the FBI, the CIA, and the ACB immediately."

"You're right," Anthony said. "But who the heck is the ACB?"

"Any cat with a badge, my man," Kwami said, giving

himself five again. "Any cat with a badge."

"What you're saying is that we better turn over all our evidence to the authorities, right?" Kitty said.

"Right," Kwami said, "and it only took you longer than anyone else to figure that out."

"Uh-huh." Kitty still had her sideways look on. "And what evidence do we have?"

"What evidence?" Kwami asked. He stood up slowly and looked at Kitty. "We know the dude is a spy, or he wouldn't be messin' with those Russians. That's what evidence."

"Evidence is what you have you can show people, Kwami," Kitty continued. "What do you have that you can show Willie is guilty?"

"How about all the times we seen him with them Russians, that's evidence," Anthony said.

"How about those envelopes those Russians had coming out of Willie's place?" I said.

"You got a picture of any of that stuff?"

"Wow, you can tell he's a spy," Wayne said. "Look how slick he was in hiding all the evidence."

"Maybe he'll confess."

"They get him downtown and give him the third degree," Judy said.

"What's the third degree?" Wayne asked.

"That's when they beat you up so you can't tell if you were beat up," Kwami said. "They pound on you with telephone books and rubber hoses and stuff."

"He might have a poison capsule like that cat on television that comes on right after Merv Griffin," Anthony said.

"I think we needs to go back and get us some evidence," Kwami said. " 'Cause right now all we got is suspicion."

"Back where?" Judy asked.

"Back to Willie's place."

"I ain't going back," Judy said. "I don't care what nobody says. I ain't going back and get fixed again."

"Dean got to go!" Kwami said.

"I ain't going!" I said. "I'm the one she put down that blood and stuff for. If I went I wouldn't have a chance, man! You got to be crazy!"

"Well, if he don't go I know I'm not going!" Kitty got up from where she was sitting and shook her finger at me. "We're all your friends and everything but now's the time that you got to take some risks, too. How would I feel going down there and getting fixed and maybe dying and everything and you're up here drinking a pineapple soda?"

"The reason that somebody else has to go," I said, putting down the pineapple soda, "is that she put a special curse on the place just for me. If I go I'm a goner."

"If you're brave enough you might be able to defy her curse," Leslie said.

"I ain't brave enough!"

"You got to be a man, Dean."

"Right, and if I go down there I'll die a boy. Why don't you go down there?"

"Okay, I got an idea," Kwami said. "Let's nobody go down there. Let's just all sit here and maybe another idea will come to us."

Everybody sat down on the stoop.

"Hey, Wayne," Kwami called out to Wayne louder than he had to. "Did you see the Knicks play Philadelphia the other night, man? Bob McAdoo looked so sweet I thought he was me!"

"No, I didn't see the game," Wayne said. "I had to do my homework because Mrs. Goldstein double-crossed me and sent a note home to my mother."

"Yeah? What teacher is she?" Kwami asked, wiping off the mouth of my pineapple soda.

"Social studies," Wayne replied.

"Umm." Kwami nodded while the bottle was still draining into his mouth. We watched as all of the soda disappeared down his bobbing throat. Finally, he spoke to Wayne. "Social studies teachers are like that," he said. "What do you think about them clouds up in the sky?"

"The clouds?" Wayne asked.

"Yeah, the clouds, man," Kwami said. "I mean, we aren't going to get no evidence on Willie so we might as well start talking about the clouds and things like that."

"You people don't care if I die or anything," I said.

"There you go feeling sorry for yourself again," Kwami said. "Just remember, dying couldn't be too bad. People are dying today who wouldn't have even thought of dying before. Dying is definitely in."

"That's cold, Kwami."

"Hey, you know, he's right, Dean," Leslie said. "If we're going to risk getting fixed, you should at least come along."

"No, leave him alone," Kwami said. "We can just sit here on the stoop with him until it's over."

"I'll go, man." I said. "But if I'm the only one that dies, just remember I told you so."

Leslie didn't have any fresh garlic so she put some dehydrated garlic in a small bag and hung it around my neck to ward off any undead who were hanging around in human form. I told them that I would try to go by myself first, but if I couldn't make it, I'd come back to get someone to go with me. Kwami and Leslie volunteered to be lookouts, and Wayne and Judy watched at the window.

I shook everyone's hand, and Judy kissed me on the cheek, and then I went down the backstairs to Willie's place. I stood near Willie's door for a minute before I put the toe of my sneaker against it and pushed gently. The door opened without a sound. I looked toward the window where Wayne and Judy sat. Wayne waved and Judy just looked at me. I pushed the door slowly open.

It was cool in Willie's place and the dampness made the air hard to breathe. We had seen Willie and Drusilla go into Willie's place with the Russians an hour before, and I was going to try to get some kind of real evidence on Willie. I could see a light coming from beneath a door down the hallway and the sound of low voices. Otherwise it was dark in the basement. I didn't like moving around in the darkness, but at least if somebody came out of the room quickly they wouldn't be able to see me. I moved slowly along the wall, lifting my feet barely off the ground so as not to make much noise. I got caught up in a spiderweb for a minute and had to stop to brush it off my face. It reminded me of the roach that had crawled on Wayne.

Just ahead of me there was a scurrying sound and the grey form of a rat darted across the patch of light toward me. It stopped suddenly and I couldn't see it, but I imagined it to be just a few feet in front of me. I thought that it might have run into a hole. The scurrying noise came again, quick scratching on the broken cement floor. I could see the rat again, huddled near the light, its head stretched as high as it could reach with all four paws still on the ground. I could see its form, but I could only see one of its eyes shining. I stood perfectly still. The rat moved slowly toward me, until it wasn't in the light. I couldn't see it for a while and then I felt it moving across the toe of my sneaker. A trickle of cold sweat ran down the side of my face.

Suddenly, a piercing scream filled the basement and echoed in the darkness. The rat ran halfway up my pants leg and then leapt away in the darkness as I jumped back. I started to turn toward the door I had come in but I didn't know the way somehow. I knew I just had to follow the wall. I slid my hands along the rough surface and felt something soft and furry. I grabbed it with both hands, afraid of knowing and not knowing what it was all at the same time. I felt it frantically in the darkness until I figured out that it was just an old coat that someone had hung on a nail in the wall. It had come off the nail as I was feeling it and I found the nail and hung it back up. I told myself not to panic and it seemed almost funny because I was panicking. I took a couple of deep breaths and started to move back toward the light. My knee began to throb and I figured I must have banged it into the wall when I jumped.

The scream had come from the room that the light came from. I really didn't want to get any closer, but I could feel my legs still moving slowly. As I got nearer the door I could hear what sounded like chanting. I couldn't make much of what was being said. I listened carefully. There was no noise other than the chanting. It was low, as if someone were chanting the words to a song that didn't have much of a melody. There was a window on the other side of the room which had been the opening for a flue for the coal burner before the building had changed to oil. Willie had put some plastic over it and some curtains. I made my way over to it and found that I couldn't see through the curtains. There was a small sliver of light at the top of the window and I began to feel around in the darkness for something to stand on, all the while listening to the chanting that came steadily from the room. I found a paint can and brought it over to the window, turning it upside down before standing on it.

Drusilla sat at the head of the table and a white man, probably a Russian, I thought, sat at the other end. There were two more Russians standing with Willie against the wall. They were the same ones that I had seen in the limousine before. The one sitting across from Drusilla I had never seen. He was older than the others. His hair was almost completely white and his beard grew like a large grey bush from his face. I couldn't tell what his face looked like.

In front of Drusilla there was a chicken, its legs tied together and a bag over its head. At first, I thought that it was dead, but every once in a while it would move. It was Drusilla who chanted as she held the candle over the chicken.

"Du Avee Messee   Du Avee Messee   Du Avee Messee   Bebe de sol okeh   Bebe de sol okeh   Bebe de sol okeh."

There was a candle near the chicken and each time Drusilla chanted, her thin, brown hands would go slowly through the flames. She was not looking at the flames or the chicken. Her head was back, the glow of the candle flickering on her neck like demons trying to force their way from her throat.

"Du Avee Messee   Du Avee Messee   Du Avee

Messee   Bebe de sol okeh   Bebe de sol okeh   Bebe de sol okeh."

She pulled the bag from the chicken's head and it immediately began to try to stand. She held it with one hand while she untied its feet. The white man opposite her clasped his hands together and then opened them and placed them palms down on the table. Drusilla pulled the chicken to her bosom and continued the chant. I don't know where she got the knife from. I saw the blade of the knife shine in the light of the candle. The chicken beat its wings furiously as the blade entered the dark brown feathers. The feathers grew darker with the blood of the chicken and it went limp in Drusilla's hands.

"Du Avee Messee!"

Her voice rose and her body jerked upward from the chair.

"Du Avee Messee!"

Her eyes opened wide and she began to look around as if she were afraid.

"Du Avee Messee! Du Avee Messee! Du Avee Messee!"

What had begun as a chant now seemed like the scream that I had heard in the hallway. Drusilla's body jerked violently until she fell out of the chair. She sat up on the floor. Willie started to go to her, but one of the Russians held him back. Drusilla started jerking again and her arms began to twitch. She looked around, as if trying to find someone to help her. Suddenly the jerking began again and her arms twitched and I saw that she looked just like the chicken she had plunged the knife into seconds before. She flopped about the floor. There was blood on her chest above the dark house-coat she wore, but I couldn't see if she was wounded. Her arms and legs crashed hard into the legs of the table and chair. She was trying to get up, but she couldn't quite make it. Her voice was getting higher and higher.

"Du Avee Messee! Du Avee Messee! Du Avee Messee!"

It seemed to come from deep within her. She managed to get to her knees. She reached up and pulled the dead chicken down to her. She held it to her bosom and rocked from side to side as she sat near the leg of the table on the floor. She was beginning to be calmer now.

"Du Avee Messee   Du Avee Messee   Du Avee Messee   Bebe de sol okeh   Bebe de sol okeh   Bebe de sol okeh."

Once again it was more like a chant. Drusilla got up from the floor and sat on the chair. She held the chicken to her bosom as she repeated the chant. Then, without warning, she threw the chicken across the room. It landed in a corner. I looked at Drusilla. She was fixing her dress. Her face had returned to calm. There was a clucking noise. I turned to where the chicken had lain a moment before and saw it standing.

I jumped down from the paint can and edged my way along the wall back to where I had come in. It seemed like forever in the pitch darkness but finally I got to the door. I opened it and felt the warm spring night breeze against my skin. I sucked in a deep breath and got out of the backyard as soon as I could.

"But I don't understand one thing." Judy sat cross-legged on the floor in Leslie's living room. "What were the Russians doing there?"

"I think the whole thing is going down soon," Kwami said as he folded his sweat socks carefully over the tops of his sneakers. "We only saw two Russians before, right?"

"Right," Wayne answered.

"Okay." Kwami rested his elbows on his knees. "Now all of a sudden Dean sees a third Russian. He's got to be the boss, see? Plus Drusilla, who we have never actually seen with the Russians before, is on the scene doing something with a chicken."

"A sacrifice," Leslie said. "She's making a sacrifice."

"Why?" Judy shifted uncomfortably.

"Because the whole thing is going to go down soon," Kwami repeated. "The top Russian came in with the plans. Whatever it is that Willie has to do up at the laboratory he has to do it soon."

"And Drusilla sacrificed a chicken to protect him," Leslie added.

"But the chicken wasn't dead," I said. "At least I don't think it was . . . you know . . . at first I thought it was dead and then . . . . "

"When Drusilla was on the floor she had taken the

soul of the chicken. That's why she was holding it to her bosom," Leslie said. "When she came out of that spell the chicken was alive again, except that it doesn't have a soul. It's dead and it's not dead."

"The more I hear about this, the less I want to hear," added Kitty. "Now you mean all the meetings that Willie was having with the Russians and everything were all leading up to whatever it is they're going to do now?"

"That's right," Kwami said. "And whenever Drusilla finishes whatever she's doing with the Russians she's probably going to finish her business off with you."

"Maybe she forgot about me," I said, hopefully. It seemed to me that the more I tried to get out the deeper I was getting in this whole mess. When we first started out, I just hit Drusilla a little with my bicycle. Now the Russians were involved, Drusilla had threatened to get me, and wherever you turned there was blood.

There was the blood that Leslie was trying to fix Major with in the park. And who was there watching the whole thing? Me.

Then there was the blood that Drusilla was spreading around Willie's house to get the last person in the house. And who was the last person? Me.

And then there was all that blood with that chicken down in the basement. Right. There I was watching the whole thing.

"The only one who has any real evidence," Judy was

saying, "is Dean. 'Cause he saw Drusilla actually doing that chicken in."

"Right," Kitty chimed in with her two cents. "And he saw her messing with that photograph when he was over to her house, too."

"I don't think she's really going to get any of us," Judy went on, "but if she does, no doubt it'll be old Dean."

"And there's nothing we can do about it because I don't want to tempt that chick into turning me into no Kentucky Fried Zombie," Kwami said.

"There's one thing. Remember I was telling you about how Mojo people get the undead to do their bidding?"

"Yeah, yeah." Anthony rolled his eyes toward the ceiling.

"Well, if you reach across a grave and touch an undead person, you can get what they call a Mojo hand over your own hand. Once you got that Mojo hand you can do one Mojo stronger than anybody else in the whole world. If it's strong enough you can get any spell off of anybody. If it's not, there's nothing else you can do in the world."

"Mama Doc, ain't no use in you feeling bad, so why don't you go on and eat your dinner?" Drusilla watched as Mama Doc once again sniffed the pan of boiled codfish that had been prepared for her. "That fish was eighty cents a pound, Mama Doc, so don't go turning your nose up at it.

"Oh what's wrong with you anyway? Well, I don't even care, that's the way I feel. If you want to go around acting funny then go right ahead. Ever since I went over to Willie's house with them Russians you acting funny. I didn't do nothing wrong! I don't care what you think! What are you, anyway? You ain't nothing but an old black cat. You ought to be lucky you even here and getting fed every single day the Lord sends. For sure you ain't much company.

"Anyway, how you know that what they were saying wasn't true? That's the whole thing, you don't know. Willie believes it, and Willie's a human being, which is more than I can say for you, Mama Doc. Hm. The day I got to explain anything I do to an old cat will be the day when I turn my mind in for something secondhand. I *know* what I did was right. They can scribble all they want to or anything else they want to do—I don't care.

"I am so tired, Mama Doc. My legs ache something awful. Do you hear that? They just ache something awful. I got to look around for something easier to do. You know, Mama Doc, that I really didn't mean to do nothing wrong. My grandfather used to say, 'Don't be making fun in the Lord's darkness.' I wasn't making fun, Mama Doc, that's for sure. And you know I didn't take those few dollars they were so anxious to be giving out. No, child, not me. Still, I was just thinking that—Mama

Doc, are you paying attention to me? I was just wondering if I knew exactly where I was going following behind Willie?

"Did I tell you I had a bad dream? I dreamt I was someplace in the dark with my eyes open. I couldn't see a thing and I couldn't hear a thing. All there was was darkness and silence. I thought I must have been awake and I wasn't. It was a dream and it seemed that I dreamed all night long about the same thing. Sure was a funny dream, Mama Doc, wasn't it?"

Eleven

⊂▷ "When?" Judy asked.

"Last night when we went out to visit my aunt in Queens." Leslie hadn't taken her stare from Kitty's face. "My aunt lives near St. Michael's Cemetery. It must have been a new grave because the marker was still kind of shiny. A person named Scott. All of a sudden I felt this cold chill all through my hand, but I didn't move. Then slowly I felt like someone was putting a glove over my hand. And I knew I had a Mojo hand."

"We're—I mean you're—going to put a super Mojo on Drusilla?" I asked.

"Nope, on the Russians," Leslie said. "If it works, we can stop the Russians and then when Drusilla finds out what happened she'll be afraid to try anything."

"An atomic Mojo, man," Anthony chipped in.

"I'm going to try," Leslie said.

"When?" Judy asked.

"Tomorrow, before it's too late," Leslie said.

Putting a Mojo on the entire Russian Consulate wasn't the easiest thing in the world to do. Leslie didn't think that many people in the world could do it. I certainly wasn't sure she could do it.

But it was a good idea for two reasons. First, if it worked, then we could stop the Russians from doing whatever it was they were doing and second, we weren't messing around directly with Drusilla. I hadn't really slept well for almost two weeks. Every night I would dream something like being trapped in Drusilla's house or having her put a picture of me in a pot of water. By this time I just wanted to get the whole thing over. I wasn't sure that Leslie could pull off a super Mojo, but I figured it was at least worth a try.

It took nearly forty minutes for the Number Twenty bus to wind its way along One Hundred and Twenty-fifth Street and up the West Side to the end of the line at Van Cortlandt Park and Two Hundred and Forty-second Street. From there we had to walk the rest of the way to the consulate building.

The biggest problem was drawing a circle around the building. Leslie had brought along three boxes of chalk for the purpose, one of which was colored chalk, and had already decided that if we couldn't draw a complete circle around the building we could probably make do with a giant parenthesis.

"Mojo is very symbolic, you know," she said, covering her mouth slightly even though there was only one other person sitting near us on the bus. "If you take something and make a symbol of it then it's always perfect, but if you take the real thing it's never perfect."

"Nothing's perfect," Kwami said.

"Nothing except me, anyway," Judy said, a big grin spreading across her face.

"You better be serious," Leslie chided. "We're not going on a picnic, you know."

We went over the plans again, for the third time. Judy, Wayne, and Kitty were going to work on drawing the circle (or parenthesis if a circle couldn't be drawn), then we were all going to walk around the building with the lit candles and Leslie was going to put the Mojo on the consulate. Leslie had all the equipment—including the third bag of fresh chicken livers she had bought that month—in a Barnes & Noble shopping bag.

The consulate was a lot bigger than we had thought it was, even though Judy and Kitty, who had already seen it, had described it to us before. It didn't look like a very friendly building and neither did the people who went in and out of its front doors.

"I wonder how come their suits are always too big," Kitty said, nudging Judy and looking toward a man just emerging from the building.

As we got about a block away from the consulate, there were police barricades and people in gypsy clothing carrying signs reading "Freedom for Gypsies!" "Romany, not Russian!" The police were keeping them behind the barriers even though other people were free to go beyond the barriers as they wished.

We walked once around the entire building while Leslie handed out the chalk and candles. The second time we walked around, Judy and Wayne stayed on one side and Kitty stayed on the other. We were going to have to do the parenthesis after all.

While Wayne, Kitty, and Judy made their chalk marks, Leslie dipped her fingers in the chicken livers and made an X on each corner of the building. Then, just for luck, she wrote Leslie 120 on one of the corners. Then she went across the street, and sat on a bench, and recited the spell which she had typed directly from a book of spells and incantations while me, Kwami, and Anthony slowly began circling the building with lit candles. Leslie had been thoughtful enough to get candles that had burned down some so the wind didn't blow them out.

We were supposed to go around the building three times. The first time we would go slowly, the second time as quickly as possible, and the third and final time slowly again. At the end of the third time the Mojo would be complete. Things worked smoothly the first two times.

Me and Wayne were the first ones to be picked up. A policeman told us that we couldn't demonstrate that close to the consulate, and we told them that we had to if the Mojo was going to work. They also asked us what we were protesting.

"Nothing," Wayne answered the plainclothes policeman.

"Then why are you carrying that candle?" the policeman asked.

"This is a Mojo candle," Wayne answered.

The policeman, as casually as possible, got on his radio.

"SEVENTEEN THREE THIS IS BAKER TWO. DO YOU READ ME?"

"Baker Two, this is Seventeen Three. Loud and clear."

"SEVENTEEN THREE I HAVE TWO BLACK MALES ABOUT ELEVEN YEARS OLD APPARENTLY PUTTING ON SOME KIND OF PROTEST ON CORNER TWO A."

"A two-person protest, Baker Two?"

"You by yourselves?" the policeman asked.

Wayne shook his head.

"Where are the others?"

"There goes Anthony down there, and Kitty and Kwami are on the other side of the building." Wayne pointed down the street where Anthony was walking with his candle.

"SEVENTEEN THREE THIS IS BAKER TWO. THERE ARE A

NUMBER OF SUSPECTS AROUND THE CONSULATE."

"Baker Two, does the group have anything to do with the NAACP?"

"What's the name of your outfit, sonny?" the policeman asked.

"The name?"

"Yeah, what kind of operation you guys got going?"

"Oh, Operation Brother Bad," Wayne said. "Just about everybody you see with them Mojo candles is in this group. Here comes Judy now."

The cop looked down the street and saw Judy walking slowly down the street with her candles.

"SEVENTEEN THREE THIS IS BAKER TWO. THIS IS SOMETHING CALLED OPERATION BROTHER BAD AND THOSE AREN'T CANDLES—THEY'RE MOJOS."

"They're what, Baker Two?"

"MOJOS, CAPTAIN. AND THEY'RE INTERRACIALS."

"Interracial Mojos? Baker Two, I'm sending in backup units. Take suspects into custody."

Twelve

We were rounded up so fast it made my head spin. By the time that me and Wayne got to the precinct in one car, the rest of the group was already there. The precinct was full of people. Some of the gypsies had had a fight and the police had arrested them. There were some other guys there with baseball bats arguing about if some guy was safe at third base, and an Irish lady was trying to get the police to make her husband come home from Gaelic Park and spend more time with the family.

"Will somebody get these kids out of here?" The desk sergeant pointed at us with his thumb and I could see Wayne was just about ready to cry.

"These are the kids we picked up around the Russky consulate, Sarge." The policeman who had first stopped me and Wayne looked uncomfortable. "Seventeen Three said to take them in."

"Well, take them into the back and get their names or something!"

They took us all in this big room with a lot of desks and made us stand along the wall. There was a television set on with the ballgame and some of the policemen were watching that. The officer that brought us in went over and said something to one of the guys behind the desk in civilian clothes. Then he motioned for us to come over.

"I'm Sergeant Smith," he said, looking at us one by one. "And I'm not going to arrest you this time. But the next time I see any of you near the Russian, or any other consulate, you'll all go to jail for the rest of your lives, hang by your thumbs, and live on nothing but stale bread and water with little green flies in it. You all understand that?"

We nodded. He sounded a little like my father.

"Hey, Smitty, what's up?" A heavy man whose shirt was open under his tie came up with a clipboard in his hand.

"Nothing, Vinnie, everything's okay." Sergeant Smith stood up quickly and started leading us toward the door.

"Are those them interracial Mojos?" Vinnie's voice sounded as if he should be clearing his throat.

"Naw, not these kids," Smith said.

"Yes, we are," Judy said.

"You file a report downtown?" Vinnie was tapping his clipboard.

"For God's sake, Vinnie." Smith turned back toward the heavy man. "These are just a bunch of kids fooling around. They're not subversives. They're not dangerous. They're just plain old average American kids."

"What you got in that bag, honey?" Vinnie asked Leslie.

"Chicken livers," she replied.

"She's a chicken lover," Smith said.

"What are them candles for?" Vinnie asked, peering into the bag that Leslie still clutched tightly.

"They're Mojo candles." Leslie's voice was so low they could hardly hear it.

"You know what Mojo is, Smith?"

"No, Vinnie, I don't. But I do know these are just a bunch of know-nothing kids."

"You better file a report downtown."

"Do *you* know what Mojo is?" Smith asked.

"How would you feel, Smith," Vinnie asked, "if somebody came into your house with a load of chicken livers and all these candles, eh?"

"That my cat was going to have a great meal by candlelight," Smith said. "Aw, come on, Vinnie. I'm off in a half an hour and I promised the old lady I'd take her up to Yonkers to see her mother."

"If it were my bust—"

"It's not a bust—it's a—wait a minute, I'll call downtown."

Smith turned his card file until he found the number he was looking for and dialed it. The first time he got a wrong number and the second time he got through.

He spoke to some guy named Kelly and started telling him about us. Only he said it like he was really bored with the whole thing. Then he described us a little, especially Judy, and said we looked okay to him. He was carrying on two conversations, one with us and the other with the guy on the phone. Every time the guy on the phone would ask him a question he would ask us, and I guess we were giving the wrong answers because he kept acting like the answers we gave were hurting him.

"Just a minute, Joe." Sergeant Smith covered the mouthpiece of the telephone. "Where you kids from?"

"A Hundred and Twentieth Street, mostly," Dean answered.

"Except for me," Judy said. "I live between Broadway and Riverside."

"They're not neighborhood kids, Joe, but they seem all right . . . just a childish prank. You know, with television and all . . . no particular reason—they just decided to put a Mojo on the consulate. You didn't have any particular reason, did you, kids?" Sergeant Smith shook his head no and we shook ours yes.

"Well, they had a reason but . . . just a moment." He turned to Kitty. "What's the reason?"

"Because Willie who was working at the university in a top-secret job kept messing around with those Russians that came downtown all the time and we figured he was a spy, and since we saw one of the Russians on television with the President we thought we'd better do something about it." Kitty got it all out in one breath, paused, and continued: "And anyway we had to do something because Willie's girl friend was going to put a Mojo on Dean because he knocked her down with his bicycle."

"Hello, Joe? Look, I'll call you back. I got to call my wife and tell her to start defrosting something for dinner. We're not going to her mother's after all. Yeah, you heard, huh? Talk to you later."

It was two o'clock when we arrived by police car at FBI headquarters. A few people stopped to look at us, and Kwami pulled his coat over his head. I started to do the same thing but no one else did so I didn't either.

Inside we had to tell our story to four different guys who called themselves Special Agents. "I'm Special Agent So and So. Why don't you tell me all about it."

Then they would have a conference and start questioning us again. After a while they put us all in one room and told us just to relax for a while. Kwami said the room was probably bugged. Then they called us out two by two and had us look at a lot of pictures. Most of the pictures were of people I had never seen before. Judy and I were looking at the pictures together. We were about half way through a big pile of pictures when a picture of one of the Russians came up. I didn't know if I should say anything or not and I looked at Judy and she was looking right at me. A picture of the other Russian was there, too. Then they showed me three more pictures and asked me if I recognized any of them as the guy in the basement when Drusilla was putting a Mojo on the chicken. I told them that I didn't see the face so I really couldn't tell.

Judy asked who the Russians were. One of the agents said that one of them was a guy named Serge Ivanoff and that he was a sports director. We asked him what they were doing with Willie, and he said that's what the FBI was trying to find out, too. We had to go back into the room they were keeping us in before, and this time one of the agents stayed in the room with us. There was a telephone in the room and it rang after about three minutes.

The FBI guy picked up the phone, listened for a minute, and then put the phone down. He didn't say a word. Which was cool. He told us to come with him and we were led down the hall to another room. We stayed there for a while and then had to go into the elevator to the main floor. When we got off the elevator Kwami's parents, Judy's parents, Wayne's mom, and my mother were there, but the FBI guy just hustled us right past them and down the hall. Kwami's father was looking mad, as usual, and my mother was saying "what happened" only she wasn't using words, just mouthing them. I thought I had better keep my mouth shut. I wondered if they were going to get Willie and Drusilla, too. When the door opened to the room we were going to I had my answer. There were two agents questioning Willie. One was short and the other was very tall. The short one was wearing a shoulder holster and I could see the handle of his gun. Drusilla was sitting there, listening.

"I told you one time, man." Willie turned his big hands up to the ceiling. "They said they were interested in what they called a cultural exchange. They was going to give some black kids scholarships, and they wanted to know more about the kids and how to choose them. Then they found out that Drusilla had a Mojo hand and they wanted to know more about that. That didn't bother me none 'cause the only thing I was interested in was helping the kids."

"Scholarships to Russian schools?" Shoulder Holster tightened the strap on his weapon until it cut into his arm. "You mean you're trying to get American kids into Russian schools?"

"Education is education. Half these kids around here can't afford to go to college at all," Willie said. "I want some of these kids to have a chance, too."

"Well, how come the Russians didn't go to the NAACP or some other good-doing black outfit?"

"They said they thought some of those outfits were

spy fronts," Willie continued. "Anyway, I didn't even care, 'cause if some of the kids get scholarships to go to school, everything's okay with me."

"What's your girl friend got to do with all of this?" The first agent sat on the edge of the table.

"She's my lady," Willie said, sitting up a little straighter. "And they just wanted to find out how black people live so that if they sent the kids over there they'd be able to make them feel at home, that's all."

"The kids said that she tried to Tojo them," Shoulder Holster said.

"Mojo," corrected the first agent.

"Drusilla just running off at the mouth," Willie protested. "She ain't got a mean bone in her body."

"That Mojo, that's really dangerous stuff?" Shoulder Holster loosened the strap of his weapon and flexed his fingers.

"Yeah," Willie said. "Sure."

"And she was going to zap that kid with it?"

"What do you mean, zap?" Drusilla had her hands on her hips.

"Do not vorry, chentlemen." There was a rustle of activity as Constantine, Serge, and the other Russian came into the room. Constantine was smiling and I could see that most of his teeth were yellow. "Drusilla is not a real Mojo lady. She is a fake."

"Who are these guys?" Shoulder Holster turned to the agent that brought in the Russians.

"We've . . . er . . . invited some members of the

Russian consulate down to help clear the matter up."
The agent looked Shoulder Holster in the eye and Shoulder Holster sat down on the edge of a desk.

"I am sure, Villie, that you vill be released soon. The charges are obviously trumped up to embarrass you and to promote a decadent capitalistic system that is already in its last stages of decline."

"They're saying that I'm some kind of a spy!" Willie said.

"A spy? Villie cannot be a spy." Constantine turned to the FBI agents.

"And just why not," Shoulder Holster asked, sticking out his chin.

"Vell, according to our records, he did not go to your spy school in Virginia, or the vun in Ayer, or the Hollobird School, or the vun in Vhite Sands, or in . . . "

"Enough, enough." The FBI agent turned crimson.

"And, as ve said, the lady is a fake as vell."

"A what?"

"According to our Mojo expert, Dr. Tchaimainov, she is incapable of—"

"She ain't no fake," Wayne said. "Dean saw her fix a guy all the way down in Louisiana. Then he saw her kill a chicken and bring it back to life!"

"You saw that?" Constantine turned and looked at me. I tried to smile but it came out as one of my stupid smiles. "No matter, ve are not convinced."

"You ain't convinced?" Where Wayne was getting his big mouth from all of a sudden I didn't know, but he didn't even feel Leslie nudging him. "She can do all kinds of things. She was getting set to do Dean in when you people started fooling around. She can still do him in if she wants to."

"Oh?" Constantine looked over at me. "Dr. Tchaimainov says she can't."

"Do him in, Drusilla," Wayne said. "Go ahead. You can show them Russians."

"Just a minute, please." One of the agents was dialing a phone as fast as he could. "We'd like to get one of our own experts down here to observe this."

"Hey, wait a minute!" I started to protest.

"Be cool, baby, it's for your country," Leslie said.

"No, I don't want to prove nothing!" I didn't want to start crying but I could feel the tears getting ready to come. Everybody was standing around looking at me and this one agent trying to hold things up until another expert could come and see me wasted. Drusilla got up and started coming over to me and I thought I was going to pass out until she got to me and put her arms around me.

"Ain't nobody gonna hurt this little long-headed child," she said. "You all want to know things you ain't got no business to know for your own evil selves. Look at you, looking like a bunch of one-eyed cats sitting under a fish cart. Not caring who you hurt or who you scare even it be a child. You should have shame on yourselves and go home and cover your mirrors lest you see how ugly you looking."

I was so surprised I almost fell down.

"Me and Willie ain't done nothin' to harm nobody and we don't be starting now. Willie, he tryin' to help these children and you devils trying to trick him. All of you is devils!" She looked them all in the eye, one by one.

"Is these babies free to go, Mister Officer?"

"Well, yeah, I guess so." The agent who had brought the Russians in straightened his tie and straightened some papers that were on the desk. Slowly, in small groups, we left.

It wasn't quite over, though. About a week later another long black limousine pulled up in front of the stoop. This time it was the FBI.

They told us that they had been investigating Serge and Constantine for a long time, as well as Tchaimainov. It seems that the Russians had been studying Mojo and other forms of what you might call supernatural powers for years. According to the FBI's intelligence reports, they're years ahead of us in the field.

"Although many of our top people think we're making a big mistake not investigating things like ESP and Mojo more seriously, and talking to people like Drusilla, we can't get enough backing to raise the money," the agent said to us. "That Russian that attended the experiment in Willie's basement is probably one of their top people."

"You mean that they got all of Drusilla's secrets?" Kwami asked.

"No, I don't think so," the agent continued. "As far as we have been able to figure out, Mojo seems to be something you're born with. You can't learn it by watching other people or reading about it."

"Well, if they didn't get any secrets," Dean asked, "how come you came down here to talk to us?"

"Well, er, we understand that your group was putting a Mojo on the Russian Embassy when you were apprehended. Is that right?"

"An atomic Mojo, too," Wayne put in.

"Well, it seems as if they've been having a little trouble and, for diplomatic reasons, we'd like you to come up and . . . you know . . . take it off? The Russians are a little nervous about the whole thing."

And that's the way it ended. With Kwami, Judy, Kitty, Wayne, Anthony, and me all following Leslie around the Russian Embassy taking off the atomic Mojo we had put on it before. We were guarded by FBI agents, none of whom believed in Mojo. But some of them did carry little cloves of garlic in bags around their necks, just in case.

ABOUT THE AUTHOR

Walter Dean Myers, a New Yorker, is the author of many magazine articles and works of short fiction; he has also written several books for children. His first novel for young people, *Fast Sam, Cool Clyde, and Stuff,* was an ALA Notable Book. Mr. Myers is currently at work on a new novel.